BETRAYED

at the

Beach

AN ALEX PAIGE MYSTERY

THERESA L CARTER

Contents

Chapter 1

Alex leaned over the balcony and inhaled the salty air. The waves echoed, enveloping her like a hug. Twenty-three stories below, the deck chairs looked tiny enough to fit in one of the Thorne Miniature Rooms at the Art Institute. Thinking of Chicago made her even more grateful to be on the Gulf. The air might have a bit of a chill, but it was nothing compared to what was going on back home. There, she'd be suited up like an astronaut instead of drinking a glass of vinho verde while seagulls checked her out at eye level.

The doorbell shook her from her reverie. She padded barefoot through the open sliding glass door, past the fireplace, past the open kitchen, down the hallway. She opened the door without looking through the peephole. She knew who it was.

"Darling!" William exclaimed and swooped Alex into his arms. He pulled back, put a hand on either shoulder, then looked her up and down. "You look absolutely fabulous." He kissed her on both cheeks, then ran his fingers through her hair. He was one of very few people allowed to do that.

"Why thank you, handsome. So do you." She peered around his shoulder. "Where's Billy? I thought he was coming with you."

William bent down, picked up his bag, and took Alex's hand as she led him into the condo. "Trouble in River City. Somebody vandalized Amelia."

"What? That's terrible," Alex exclaimed. "But investigating boat damage is a little below Billy's paygrade, isn't it? Besides, I thought he was retiring to live the nomad life with you." Alex pulled a glass from the cabinet and poured her friend some wine.

"He's doing a favor for Juke," William explained. William and Alex had met Juke the previous summer during a press trip to Door County that had turned disastrous.

To hear that someone had vandalized Juke's beloved charter boat, Amelia, dismayed Alex. "Does Billy have any idea who did it?"

William shrugged. "You know he doesn't talk shop with me. At least not intentionally," he winked. "I'm sure they'll get to the bottom of it." He took a sip of his wine. "Ah, so crisp. Good choice, m'lady. As long as Amelia doesn't get to the bottom of Lake Michigan."

Alex smiled, shaking her head, a frequent gesture around William. It had been a couple of months since the friends had seen each other. The two travel writers often attended the same press trips, but lately they'd had different assignments. On this visit to Gulf Shores, Alabama, Alex planned to combine pleasure with business. She loved her job, which was basically to go places and write about them, but it was a lot of work and she always went straight home after the official visit was done. She desperately needed some time off and had decided to extend her stay on the Gulf. She just hoped she could actually relax.

"Can you do it?" William asked, interrupting her thoughts. "Can you actually relax for a few days?"

"Mind reader," she replied. "I'm certainly going to try. I haven't had a vacation, a real vacation, in years."

"Hazard of the job."

"But what a hazard to have. My plan is to read, soak in that hot tub on the balcony, drink anything with an umbrella, and eat bon bons."

"Sounds delightful. Maybe I'll stay, too," William grinned.

"Absolutely not. I love you, but I want to be all by myself for a while." Alex took her glass and walked out to the balcony, leaning over the railing as she had been before William arrived. He followed her and the two stood silently watching the rhythmic dance of the waves far below.

She felt rather than saw William shift his gaze to her. "How have you been?" he asked. "I mean, really been."

Alex seesawed her hand. "Mostly good. Sometimes bad. I've been so busy I almost feel like I'm running away. I know I can't make up for lost time, but it seems like that's exactly what I'm trying to do."

"I imagine it could feel like you lost a year of your life."

"Sometimes it feels exactly like that. But I'm here, right? I'm alive. And it wasn't all treatments and doctors appointments. Emily spoiled the heck out of me. Plus, it showed me who Ben really was. If it hadn't been something as dramatic as 'cancer,'" Alex said, using air quotes, "I wouldn't have seen what a narcissist he is. I might have ended up married to the guy."

William gasped, putting his hand over his heart. "Forfend, dear friend! I would never have let that happen. Not that I could get you to change your mind once you had it set on something, even something as vile as Benjamin Short," he shuddered.

"You and Emily probably would have kidnapped him and shipped him off to some desert island. Good thing we don't have to worry about that now, because I don't have enough bail money for you two." Alex smiled, thinking of William conspiring with Emily, her neighbor and best friend back home. Those two had only met in person a few months before, but they'd hit it off famously. Which made sense, since they were two of Alex's favorite people.

Alex's stomach grumbled; she glanced at her watch. "It's time. Shall we go eat shrimp?"

"And gator," William replied. "I'm looking forward to those kabobs LuEllen mentioned."

"Me, too. It'll be good to see her," she said, while walking back inside.

"And eat her food. I can still taste those shrimp cakes she made in Colorado Springs, in a good way." William put the back of his hand to his forehead and affected a drawl. "Makes me want to swoon like a southern belle."

Alex chuckled and set her empty wineglass in the dishwasher. William followed suit, slinging his backpack over his shoulder. They headed towards the entrance to the condo. Alex grabbed her cross-body bag from the table by the door and confirmed her camera and notebook were inside. The evening's event was the "business" part of her business and pleasure trip to the coast. Not to say it wouldn't be pleasurable. Being a travel writer certainly had its benefits, and attending openings of restaurants in ocean-front locations was one of them.

This time, she'd also be supporting a friend. Alex and William had met LuEllen Devereaux the previous fall during a press trip to the Pikes Peak region. Now LuEllen had invited them to attend the grand opening of her second LuEllen's Shrimp Shack location. William, who focused on outdoor adventures for national publications, turned it into an opportunity to camp at Gulf State Park and explore the region. Alex wanted to dive into the history of the area. She was particularly excited to see an ancient canal dug by Archaic period peoples around 600 C.E. Those kinds of discoveries made her skin tingle.

Instead of exiting the high-rise condo building towards the street, Alex led them to the beach. They followed a boardwalk, already hearing steel drums and laughter. A young woman in board shorts and a bikini top stood up, admiring the sand sculpture she'd just completed. It was LuEllen's logo of a smiling shrimp with an arrow designed to look like a neon sign. Alex pulled her camera out of her bag; William unzipped the side of his backpack and did the same. They took a few photos. The young woman saw them and began to walk out of frame. "No, stay, if you don't mind us taking your picture," Alex said. "Do you have a card? We're travel writers."

She pulled a card out of her dry bag. As Alex neared, she realized the woman was much younger than she thought. Alex glanced at the card. Zoe Monroe, Sand Artist. "Hi Zoe, nice to meet you. We have to get to LuEllen's," she said, gesturing down the boardwalk, "but I'm here for the next two weeks. I'd love to talk to you sometime. This is fabulous," Alex said, pointing to the sculpture.

Zoe grinned, making her look even younger. "I'd love that. You can usually find me around here, but give me a call. Have fun tonight," she said.

As Alex and William continued walking towards the sound of Zydeco, William shook his head. "You're hopeless."

"Whatever do you mean?"

"I'm here for two weeks. I'd love to talk to you," he mimicked. "There is no way you're going to take any time to relax. You're going to be interviewing everyone you meet. Hopeless, I tell you."

Alex punched him lightly in the arm. Her stomach grumbled again and she picked up her pace. "We're getting close. I can smell it."

They rounded a slight bend and walked through an opening in a wall of seagrass. The volume of the music increased exponentially, as did the buzz of conversation. A one-story building made of what looked like reclaimed wood was surrounded by sand and palm trees. People dressed in sundresses and shorts flowed in and out of the open garage doors, while servers wearing red straw brimmed hats, red Bermudas, and white polos sporting LuEllen's smiling shrimp logo embroidered above the left breast milled about with trays of drinks and appetizers. The band, with its trio of steel drums, entertained from a shaded bandstand. Brightly painted picnic tables lined up on the sand, and clusters of Adirondack chairs and bamboo furniture circled stone firepits. A group of teenagers played bags. William stopped, a huge grin plastered on his face. "This is fabulous. The red. The white. The shrimp. Although why do restaurants use the animals they're serving as logos? Kind of creepy, if you think about it."

Alex shook her head. "I'm hungry, I'm thirsty, and I can see LuEllen right over there," she said, tugging William with one hand and pointing towards a short woman with puffy white hair and wire-rimmed glasses.

"Who's that other woman?"

"You know that's Harriet, you goof."

"But it can't be. That woman is smiling. And laughing. She looks, dare I say it, happy. Harriet is smiling. And that man next to her—"

"Paul."

"--is smiling, too. I have no idea how to process this."

Alex tugged William's hand. "Let's say hi." They crossed the beach, threading their way through crowds of people towards LuEllen, fellow travel writer Harriet, and Paul, a chef they'd also met in Colorado Springs. On the way, William snagged a couple of mini shrimp po' boys from a server, passing one to Alex.

"This is delicious," she said, wiping a stray dollop of remoulade from the side of her mouth.

"Next time I'll grab a whole tray, because that little two-bite tease was not nearly enough."

"It certainly wasn't."

"Gulf Coast Sunset?" a server asked, proffering a tray of drinks as they passed.

"Don't mind if we do," William said, grabbing a couple cocktails. They reached a small cluster of people whose attention focused on LuEllen.

"Alex!" the white-haired woman exclaimed. "You made it! You too, you rascal," she said, embracing them, barely managing to hug them both with her short arms. Alex smiled at Harriet over LuEllen's shoulder. Harriet smiled back. *William was right*, Alex thought; it was discomfiting. LuEllen finally released them and took one of each of their hands. "Come with me. I want you to meet someone."

The older woman was every bit the force of nature Alex remembered. She turned back to Harriet and called, "We'll catch up later." Harriet pulled her eyes away from Paul long enough to nod an acknowledgement. She was still smiling.

LuEllen led them towards one of the clusters of outdoor furniture. She stopped briefly to grab a couple of hors d'oeuvres from a passing server. "Here. Try this."

Alex took what looked like a beignet, but instead of powdered sugar, it was dusted with some kind of savory seasoning. She and William tapped their fried dough squares together, then each took a bite. William's eyes rolled into the back of his head. "Holy moly that's delicious. And hot. You, please, I'm begging you," he said, waving to a passing server and grasping for a clear cup filled with crushed ice and what looked like iced tea. He took a huge sip and his eyes bugged out even more. "Oh you," he said to the drink. "I like you."

LuEllen laughed. "You wanted gator, you got gator," she drawled. "That there's my signature Gator Gumbo Bite. It's the app that bites back."

Alex wiped tears from her eyes, nodding when a server asked her if she wanted a beverage also. "You're not kidding. I thought you liked us," she said, then took a sip. From William's reaction to his first drink, she had an idea the cocktail also packed a punch. One swallow and she knew she was right. The "iced tea" tasted suspiciously like peaches and bourbon—lots of bourbon.

"That there's my version of sweet tea. It'll cool what ails ya.'"

"Enough of those and you won't have any ails, or cares, whatsoever," Alex choked. "And yet, I need another one, both the beignet and the drink."

LuEllen winked. The trio neared a couple sitting with their backs to them in a rattan couch that faced the ocean. The man's arm rested lightly over his companion's shoulders. He said something and the woman tilted her head back and laughed, a throaty trill that was somehow hearty and delicate at the same time.

LuEllen tugged gently on the woman's braid. "Cassidy, Reid, the friends I told you about are here."

The couple stood up and turned together, and Alex swore on her cat's sixth toe she was looking at a movie poster. Tanned, toned, blonde, they were like a pair of cougars. Cassidy smiled, revealing perfect white teeth with incisors just a touch too long. "You must be Alex and William," she purred, and reached out her hand. Alex shook it, surprised to feel callouses on the stunning woman's palm.

"And I must be in heaven," William said, shamelessly eyeing Reid from head to toe, settling on a point just above the v of his white V-neck t-shirt.

Reid laughed and nudged Cassidy. "Careful honey. You may have some competition."

Cassidy eyed Alex and winked. "With both of them."

LuEllen stood off to the side and grinned. "Cassidy is my younger—much younger—sister. Reid is her..."

"Partner," Cassidy finished.

"I wasn't sure they could make it, but they surprised me. And for a reason I think will interest both of you, but particularly you, Alex," LuEllen said.

Cassidy nodded. "We'd hoped to come to the opening, but with our work, our schedules are often uncertain. However, when we found out about the medallion, we knew we had to be here."

Alex tilted her head and raised her eyebrows. "Medallion?"

A man so thin he resembled a stalk of bamboo approached LuEllen and whispered in her ear. "I'm sorry, but I have to attend to something," LuEllen said. "I'll send food and drinks over so you can talk."

Cassidy smiled at her sister and gestured to the furniture group where she and Reid had been sitting. "Shall we?" Before they could sit down, a server placed a tray with a variety of appetizers and cocktails on the table that was positioned in the middle of the couches and chairs. The couple sat, reinforcing Alex's impression of them as lithe felines. She'd never seen anyone so graceful in her life, except for William. From the muscles that expanded and contracted with every motion, she could tell they were also strong. She wondered what they did, and figured she was about to learn.

Chapter 2

R eid leaned forward, resting his elbows on his knees. "LuEllen tells us you're travel writers. You travel the country in your campervan and focus on the outdoors," he said, looking at William, then shifted his eyes to Alex. "And you travel everywhere, but you're particularly keen about history."

"She told you correctly," Alex said. "I believe learning the story behind a place helps you understand what it is today. It provides context."

Cassidy put her drink on the table and pointed at Alex. "Exactly. That's what interests us as well. We're, I suppose you'd say we're treasure hunters."

"But not in the traditional sense," Reid said, smiling at his partner, his teeth momentarily blinding Alex.

"Oh?" William prompted, completely focused on the man with the physique of a superhero sitting across from him.

Alex nudged him. "You're drooling," she whispered.

"Can you blame me?" he said out of the side of his mouth. The other couple laughed. *How can these two be real?* Alex wondered.

"We hunt for artifacts left by the original inhabitants of the Americas," Cassidy said. "We try to tell their stories, to bring to life the civilizations that existed here before Europeans arrived and destroyed their world."

"We've got a bit of Creek in our blood," LuEllen said, returning from the brief emergency that required her attention. She sat down next to Cassidy, forcing the couple to scoot over to make room, "so Cassidy takes it personally."

Cassidy's eyes flashed. "It's more than just personal. You know that."

LuEllen patted her sister's leg like the grandmother she resembled. "It wasn't an insult, Cass. I'm merely saying you're invested."

"Invested in what?" Harriet said, appearing behind LuEllen, a skewer laden with shrimp, red peppers, and zucchini in one hand, her other entwined with the man standing next to her.

LuEllen craned her neck, then motioned the couple to join them. Harriet and Paul sat in chairs on opposite sides, completing the conversation circle around the table of appetizers. Alex looked back and forth between the two. The last time she'd seen either of them had been in Colorado Springs, when she'd been certain he was a murderer. It turned out he was simply awkward, which made him a perfect match for Harriet. Inwardly, Alex blushed at the thought. A year ago she never could have imagined tolerating Harriet for any length of time. Now, she thought they might, eventually, become friends.

William squeezed Alex's knee. "You're staring," he whispered. Everyone laughed. William was the worst whisperer in the history of whisperers.

"Telling the stories of people who, for whatever reason, can't tell their own," Reid said, answering Harriet. He leaned back on the couch and trailed his fingers across the nape of Cassidy's neck. Alex swore she could feel the shivers she knew the other woman must be experiencing. The man was like a buff mashup of Brad Pitt and George Clooney, all gorgeousness and charm.

Alex felt William's head snap up. "I'm sorry to interrupt, but who are those two?"

The group swiveled as one to follow his pointing finger. "Crap," LuEllen muttered.

"Why is *she* here? Why are *they* here?" Cassidy asked, glaring at her sister.

LuEllen stood and brushed out the wrinkles in her pants. She spoke to Cassidy while watching a couple, led by a much older man, approach them. "They're the ones who discovered the medallion."

"Medallion?" Harriet asked, turning to Alex for answers. Alex shrugged. They hadn't gotten to that part yet.

Cassidy exploded out of her seat. "I knew it." She turned to Reid, who stood up slowly. "I told you it was them. Now I know—." Reid touched a finger to her lips, then put his hands on her shoulders and waited until she calmed down. She closed her eyes and breathed deeply. By the time she opened them, everyone else was standing. Cassidy turned up the corners of her mouth in a semblance of a smile. She squeezed one of Reid's hands and he removed them from her shoulders.

"OK?" he asked.

She nodded. "I'll play nice. For you, Lu," she said to her sister. "This night is about you."

Alex watched the new arrivals. The woman, a tall brunette with sweeping curls, wore a cocktail dress and stilettos, an outfit more appropriate for a restaurant with a wine cellar than a "shack" on the beach. She walked on her toes to avoid sinking into the sand. The man next to her wore an open-necked white oxford and slick-looking slacks; he steadied her with his hand on her elbow. Leading them, the older man sported a Hawaiian shirt and white linen pants. He repeatedly pulled his glasses off, polished them, then returned them to his face. While the statuesque couple moved languidly, like a drawl, the short man reminded Alex of a hummingbird. Even when the three stopped to speak with someone who'd addressed them, he seemed like he was in constant motion.

"Dr. Baker," LuEllen said, reaching out to him with both hands, which he clasped. "It's so good of you to make it. I wasn't sure you'd be able to with your big opening coming up."

"I wouldn't miss this. And please, it's Harold. We've known each other long enough, haven't we?"

LuEllen laughed, a flirtatious giggle. "If you insist, Harold," she said, trying it out. She seemed to remember they weren't alone and cleared her throat. "I'd like you to meet my sister, Cassidy, and Reid McKinley, her partner."

Cassidy reached out to shake his hand. "I've been following your research for quite some time. Your conclusions about the early Europeans are intriguing."

A shadow crossed Dr. Baker's face before he resumed smiling. "I must give credit where credit is due," he said, gesturing to the couple next to him. "Much of it was informed by the work these two have done. Their discoveries have been eye-opening." Alex caught the other couple exchange a smirk before he continued. "Forgive me; I'm being quite rude. Please allow me to present Dr. Gerald Price and Dr. Vanessa Sterling. Their research into the Spanish presence in the 16th century Americas is groundbreaking."

"Literally," Gerald said, laughing. "We're archaeologists," he explained.

Alex saw Cassidy clench her fists. Reid slid his hand over hers and she relaxed slightly. LuEllen completed the introductions, finishing with Alex, who reached out and shook the three doctors' hands. "We've heard something about a medallion," she said. "I take it it has something to do with the conquistadors?"

"You're clever," Gerald said, looking her up and down. Alex refrained from covering her chest. She was still occasionally self-conscious because it was uneven after her lumpectomy, but she was trying to move past that. This was her body now, and she wanted to embrace the proof of her survival rather than be embarrassed by it. Plus, she couldn't understand in this day and age why so many men thought such blatant appraisal was appropriate.

Vanessa glared at her husband. "It's pretty obvious, Gerald, to anyone paying a modicum of attention to the *conversation*," she said, emphasizing the last word.

He grinned unabashedly, a disarming smile that displayed a deep dimple in his left cheek. "Now now, my dear. What's obvious to you isn't obvious to everyone. Not all of us are literal geniuses."

Mollified, at least temporarily, Alex guessed, Vanessa explained. "You are correct. The medallion proves incontrovertibly that de Soto's expedition made it to these shores. We discovered it—" Cassidy coughed and Alex caught Reid subtly squeezing his partner's hand. Vanessa glared at the tan blonde and continued. "We discovered it not too far from here. I won't go into the details; that's for Dr. Baker and the opening exhibition at his museum on Saturday."

Gerald gave his wife a searching look. While Vanessa made no movement, he must have seen something, because he continued. "With Dr. Baker's permission, you're all invited to the opening."

Dr. Baker, who'd been focused on cleaning a spot on his glasses, put them back on his face and nodded vigorously. "Oh, yes, yes, please do. All of you. That's part of why I'm here, besides celebrating your opening, LuEllen, of course that's the main reason, your opening, I mean." The little man blushed, a red that flushed his throat and made him resemble a bird even more. He reached into the pocket of his Hawaiian shirt and pulled out cards, distributing them to everyone present except for the other doctors.

Alex accepted one. "De Soto in Alabama: Bringing Civilization to the Gulf." She bristled. While she hadn't done any official research into the Spaniard, she knew he had been brutal, destroying communities in his wake. *There was nothing civilized about him,* she thought. Below the title of the exhibition was an image of the medallion: in the center of an elaborate gold circle edged with filigree, a depiction of a cougar looked back at her with pearl eyes and inlaid mother-of-pearl lips. Alex shifted her gaze to Cassidy, reminded of her initial thought that she and Reid resembled the large cat. Cassidy glared at the image, her mouth open, about to speak. She met Reid's eyes. His mouth had formed a thin, angry line. Some unspoken communication passed between the two, and they turned to face Vanessa and Gerald as one. At that moment, Cassidy looked distinctly feral, her incisors ready to tear into the archaeologists.

Harriet handed the card back to Dr. Baker. "I'm afraid we'll have to decline. Paul and I are heading to D.C. tomorrow. He's scouting the next location for *Dining + Destinations*. It's a new travel cooking show," she beamed proudly, throwing Alex for another loop. She didn't know if she'd ever get used to seeing Harriet smile, but she hoped so. "He and his sister run it."

"Give Stellar my love," LuEllen said, then turned to the doctors to explain. "Stellar was a judge at the first show. Paul started out as a contestant, but turns out the rascal is a Dixon, of Dixon Kitchens, so now he's the show's location scout and primary liaison. Dixon Kitchens is responsible for this," she said, sweeping her arm around her new restaurant.

Cassidy smiled at her sister, her claws retracted for the moment. "*You* are responsible for this," she said. "They just saw a good thing and leapt at it."

Paul spoke for the first time. "She's right about that. Besides, if we didn't invest, I think you would have turned us into one of your kabobs."

Everyone laughed, dispelling the tension. The distinctive strains of Wagner's die Valkyrie broke into the laughter. Gerald reached into his pocket and handed a phone to Vanessa. In her slinky dress, she had no place to put it. She looked at the screen. "I'm sorry; we have to take this. Please excuse us."

Cassidy watched them walk to the boardwalk. Vanessa's mincing steps made her look like an awkward seagull. Cassidy breathed in through her nose, out through her mouth, and turned her attention to the museum director. "Dr. Baker, would it be possible for Reid and me to get a preview of the exhibition? We'd love to dig into it before the public is invited."

"Dig in," William guffawed. Cassidy smiled at him.

"Of course, of course. Would ten work? I can give you a quick tour. It truly is fascinating."

"When we heard about the medallion, we knew we had to see it," Reid said. "All prior research shows de Soto's expedition didn't come within two hundred miles of here."

Dr. Baker took off his glasses again and began feverishly polishing them with a handkerchief he'd pulled from his pants pocket. "Yes, yes, that's the conventional wisdom, the standard story, I daresay. That's what makes this, ahem, this discovery so remarkable."

"Discovery," Cassidy muttered under her breath. Dr. Baker looked at her sharply, his eyes narrowing. For the first time, he didn't look harried and confused, Alex thought. *Interesting.*

Chapter 3

"Dr. Baker, can you tell us more about your museum?" Alex asked. "I was planning to see it while I'm visiting the area, but I'd love to hear more from its director."

William laughed. "Told you you wouldn't be relaxing. Hopeless, I say. Hopeless."

"Am not. I plan to work for a week, then relax for a week."

"Uh-huh. Sure. We'll see," William scoffed, then gestured to Dr. Baker. "But yes, please, we'd love to hear more about your museum."

LuEllen excused herself to attend to her other guests. Reid pulled over a chair from another cluster for Dr. Baker and the group sat around the table of appetizers, which had been replenished during their conversation. Dr. Baker drummed his fingers together, removed his glasses, then put them back on. "I've always been fascinated by the assignment of curses to inanimate objects. I've collected examples of these objects from all over the globe, and several from the Americas, specifically Central America.

"Is that how you connected with those two?" Alex asked.

"No, no, I've known Gerald for years. He was one of my students at Remington University. Brilliant young man. Not nearly as brilliant as his wife. He wasn't kidding when he said she was a literal genius."

Cassidy snorted. Dr. Baker inhaled as if to reply when Gerald appeared next to him. "Hey, I heard that," Gerald said, smiling. "It's true, though. Vanessa's definitely the smart one." He squeezed Dr. Baker's shoulder. "We do go way back. Twenty years now, isn't it?"

"Twenty-one," Dr. Baker said, momentarily still. He shrugged his shoulder, a nearly imperceptible movement. Gerald squeezed before removing his hand and sitting next to him.

"Do tell," William said, leaning forward. One of the cards Dr. Baker had distributed sat face up on the table. William pointed to it, tapping one of the pearl eyes. "What's the story behind this particular gem? What's its curse? Because if you're hosting an exhibition centered around it, there has to be a curse, right?"

Vanessa returned and sat on her husband's lap, reaching over to pluck a caprese skewer from the table. She was sitting directly across from Reid, and Alex could tell Vanessa was affording him a solid view of what was under her dress. His focus didn't waver from Vanessa's face. She winked at him.

Cassidy smiled at the brunette, but it didn't get anywhere close to her eyes. She leaned back and traced her fingers along Reid's forearm. The display seemed calculated to Alex, as if she was claiming him. "Yes, please tell us more about the curse associated with this medallion, Dr. Sterling."

"Vanessa, please, Cassidy. We know each other far too well to be formal." Alex had a feeling Vanessa meant that in an entirely different way than Dr. Baker's reply to LuEllen's use of his title.

"Very well, then, *Vanessa*. Enlighten us."

Vanessa's eyes narrowed, ever so slightly. Alex wanted to wave one of LuEllen's kabobs between them to slice through the tension, but she didn't want to take the chance either woman would grab it and stab the other. "The medallion," Vanessa began, "is the story of star-crossed lovers. A native queen took a conquistador for a lover, a conquistador from de Soto's expedition."

"As one could imagine," Gerald interrupted, "that didn't go over well."

Vanessa glared at her husband, then continued. "To put it mildly. The Spaniard gave his lover a medallion made of gold and pearls. When her tribe discovered it, they poisoned her. It was a slow-acting poison, a very painful death. And they made her lover watch. Absolutely brutal," she said with relish.

Alex glanced at Cassidy and Reid, then spoke to Vanessa. "I must confess that I've not done much research into what it takes to unearth discoveries like this."

"Unearth. Good one," William guffawed.

Alex continued as if he hadn't spoken. She was used to his interjections. "It's incredible you can tell the story, especially of a relationship, from something that's been buried for centuries. How do you know that's what happened?"

Vanessa nodded at Gerald. "There are legends," he said, "oral legends passed down from generation to generation. We hear whispers of these stories and investigate."

"And pay handsomely," Vanessa said.

"You pay?" William gasped. In his and Alex's world, you never paid for stories. "How do you know they're real? People could just make stuff up for the money."

"Exactly," Cassidy said, unable to hold back. "Which is why Dr. Sterling's and Dr. Price's *research* is often questioned."

"Once," Vanessa hissed. "*One* discovery was questioned."

"For which you were both sanctioned."

"Which was retracted," Gerald said.

"Wonder how much that cost you," Cassidy muttered, low enough that Alex and Reid were the only ones to hear her.

Vanessa bit into the cherry tomato. It burst, dripping juice and seeds down her chin. She wiped it off with a napkin, her black-painted fingernails contrasting with the white fabric. Alex had been surprised to see cloth napkins, until she'd also noticed the cups and plates were compostable and there were recycling bins placed strategically around the beach. This obvious concern for the environment made her respect LuEllen even more.

"Exactly," Vanessa said, bringing Alex back to the conversation. "The board agreed it was all a big misunderstanding. This *discovery*," Vanessa emphasized, glaring at Cassidy, "is definitive proof the expedition reached Oyster Bay."

William spoke to the museum director. "Would it be possible for us to join Cassidy and Reid tomorrow? Ms. Paige here is practically chomping at the bit to see this exhibit, and I know she'll want time to ask questions, which won't be possible at the opening." He smiled at Alex. "But I should warn you; she'll have so many questions you may want to order lunch."

Vanessa whipped her head towards Dr. Baker. "What is he talking about? The exhibit doesn't open until Saturday night. *We still have work to do*," she hissed through clenched teeth.

Dr. Baker removed his glasses, again, and polished them, again, before putting them back on his face. He cleared his throat. "I invited your colleagues to join me tomorrow morning for a preview. It, well, it can't do any harm to let them see what we've done. It's a groundbreaking–," William guffawed again, interrupting him, "er, groundbreaking discovery. And if these two, Alex and William is it? come with them, well, maybe they can drum up even more excitement, wouldn't you think? Make the opening even more spectacular?"

"I thought tickets were sold out," Gerald said, his casual delivery contradicting the glare he directed at Dr. Baker, "with the exception of the few you'd held aside for VIPs, like these lovely people."

"They are, they are, but publicity is never a bad thing, right? Scarcity and demand will extend the conversation, I think. It couldn't hurt, could it?"

Vanessa leaned back, crossing her legs with a flourish, mindless of the view she offered to anyone facing her. *Or,* Alex thought, *completely mindful of it.* Vanessa drummed her fingers on the arm of the couch, the black tips of her nails clicking on the rattan. "No, no, I think this is a good thing. We'd be happy to join you," she said to Cassidy. "We can enlighten you on *exactly* how we made this significant discovery."

Gerald shook his head and looked pointedly at his wife. "I'm sorry, my dear genius, but we're already committed tomorrow morning. Remember?"

The clicking stopped. Vanessa tore her eyes from Cassidy and met her husband's gaze. "Yes, you're right. The excitement of introducing them to our findings caused it to slip my mind. I apologize for the lapse."

Gerald patted Vanessa's knee. Alex bristled. The mercurial dynamic between the two doctors shifted like a rugby scrum. They both seemed to be vying for control; it certainly didn't feel like an easy partnership.

Vanessa uncrossed her legs, another exaggerated movement, and stood up. She smoothed her dress and waited for Gerald to stand. "Gerald's reminder of our appointment has also reminded me we still have work to attend to this evening." She shielded her eyes and squinted into the setting sun, then turned and walked up the beach on her toes until she reached the boardwalk.

"Please excuse Dr. Sterling," Gerald said. "She gets quite tense before we share our discoveries with the public."

"I wonder why," Cassidy muttered, then smiled. Once again, it failed to reach her eyes. "We'll see you both Saturday."

"Yes, you most certainly will." Gerald shook Reid's hand, the squeeze lasting a little longer than was comfortable, then turned to follow his wife.

William shuddered. "What in the world was *that* all about?"

"Good question," Harriet said, then turned to Paul. "Maybe we can delay our flight and join them tomorrow morning."

Paul started shaking his head before she finished speaking. "I know you like the intrigue, but we have to be in D.C. by early afternoon or Stellar will have our heads on a platter."

Alex and William laughed, remembering the commanding restaurateur. "You definitely do not want to upset that woman," Alex said. She turned to Cassidy, who sat on the couch with her elbows resting on her knees, her eyes focused on the sand at her feet, which were tapping like a pair of drumsticks on a snare. "I hope you don't mind we invited ourselves tomorrow."

Cassidy raised her head, shaking it quickly. "No, that's fine. It will be good. You'll probably have questions for Dr. Baker that I wouldn't think of, considering my attachment to the subject."

Before Alex could ask what she meant, Dr. Baker stood up abruptly. He tugged the hem of his Hawaiian shirt, then slid his glasses to the end of his nose. His eyes darted from one to the other. "If you'll excuse me, I must also take my leave. I need to give Simon a heads up that we'll have guests tomorrow. If I don't, he'll be quite testy. He likes to have everything perfect, you see." Dr.

Baker chuckled. "My fault entirely, of course, but that's a different story. Well then, I'll see you at ten. OK." He tipped his head, pushed his glasses back up, then slogged through the sand towards LuEllen. Alex watched as he grasped the white-haired woman's hand with both of his, then leaned forward and awkwardly kissed her on the cheek. LuEllen looked up, catching Alex's gaze, and Alex could swear the older woman blushed before she began making her way towards the group.

"Very interesting," William said in Alex's ear. "Looks like our dear Lu has a suitor."

"What? Dr. Baker? No, that's not possible," Cassidy said, watching her sister approach.

Reid patted her hand. "I'm afraid it's entirely too possible," he said. "I know you were caught up in the arrival of our 'friends,' but surely you noticed the interaction between the doctor and your dear sister?"

Cassidy shook her head. "Not possible," she repeated. "Lu has more sense than to fall for a charla—"

"Charming man who's obviously too old for her?" Reid interrupted. "I'm not so sure. I know you're protective of her, but she is a grown woman."

"One who raised you, I might add," LuEllen said as she reached them. "I hear you four are getting a preview? Wonderful. Be sure to take lots of notes and photos and tell me all about it. Now, Harriet and Paul, please tell Stellar I may never forgive her for taking you away from me so soon," she said with a smile, then hugged them both. The group stood as one. Alex exchanged numbers with Cassidy so they could coordinate the morning's visit to the museum. The archaeologists walked with LuEllen towards the open garage door and William and Alex headed towards the boardwalk leading back to the condo.

On their way out, William picked up a couple cups of LuEllen's version of sweet tea. "For the walk," he winked. He handed one to Alex, then took a sip. "I must know, my dear insightful friend. What do you make of all that kerfuffle?"

Alex didn't answer right away. The whole interchange was laced with hidden meanings and years' worth of built-up drama. "There's obviously a long-standing conflict between the doctors and Cassidy and Reid," she said. "I'm sure we'll learn more tomorrow."

"I certainly hope so," William said. "This drama drama drama could be quite interesting."

Alex paused on the boardwalk, turning towards the Gulf of Mexico. She closed her eyes and felt the last rays of the sun touch her skin. She did not want another interesting adventure. There had been enough of those in the previous year and a half to last her a lifetime. But, considering the dynamics they'd witnessed and the thick tension that surrounded Vanessa and Gerald's discovery, Alex had a feeling this visit wouldn't be the idyllic beach vacation she'd imagined.

She sighed. "That's what I'm afraid of."

Chapter 4

Cypress trees flanked the Spanish colonial house, tendrils of brown moss draping the sprawling branches. Alex shielded her eyes from the glare off the white stucco, following the contours of the building up to the red barrel roof tiles. The Gulf Coast History and Archaeology Museum was housed in a stately mansion, one that looked like it had been plucked out of a plantation. It was surrounded by estates guarded by wrought iron gates and adobe walls. A weathered plaque next to the door indicated the building was on the National Register of Historic Places, and that it had been built in the early 1860s.

Alex walked towards the twelve-foot double doors, reaching for the circular bronze knocker. As she grasped it, William moved up next to her and rang the doorbell.

"You're no fun," Alex said.

"Whatever do you mean?"

"I wanted to hear what it would have sounded like to knock on this door in the 1800s, because I'm betting this whole entry is original."

"You'd be correct," Cassidy said, joining them on the portico, Reid following closely behind her.

Alex was about to respond when Dr. Baker opened the door. The massive entryway dwarfed him, and he looked even smaller than he had the night before. Vanessa stood next to him. She swept her eyes over the quartet, landing on Cassidy. "That's right," Vanessa said. "You arranged your own little private tour this morning. I'd forgotten about that." Alex didn't believe for one second Dr. Sterling had forgotten anything. Vanessa turned to Dr. Baker and grasped his hand. "I'll have confirmation for you tomorrow morning, and we'll finalize everything after the opening." She held his hand until he nodded. "Good. Glad to see we're still on the same page." She let go, then spoke directly to Alex and William, ignoring Cassidy and Reid. "I will see you tomorrow evening," she said, then descended the stairs in four-inch platform sandals.

"That woman is ridiculous," Cassidy said.

"Entirely," Reid agreed, "but we're here to finally get a look at Dr. Baker's museum. We've heard so much about it, and about you, Doctor."

"Yes, welcome, welcome," Dr. Baker said, stepping aside to let them through. "I'm glad to show you around. You're right on time. OK, then. Shall we? I hope you'll forgive me, but we still have quite a lot to do before the opening, so we'll have to rush a bit."

Cassidy smiled at the diminutive man. "We appreciate any time you can spare, Dr. Baker. Thank you again for allowing us to see the medallion before the general public."

"It is my honor to welcome two esteemed researchers such as yourselves, as well as two respected journalists. Oh!" he said with alarm. "Please don't touch that. The oils from your hand will destroy the gilding."

William yanked his hand back. It looked like he'd been about to stroke the gold frame of a portrait of Hernando de Soto. "Apologies. It was like a magnet; my hand took on a life of its own," he said, wiggling his fingers.

Dr. Baker extracted a handkerchief from his pocket and wiped his forehead. "That happens here, I'm afraid. It's why nearly everything's under glass and behind ropes."

"Especially the cursed items, right?" Reid said.

Dr. Baker nodded vigorously. "Oh yes, definitely. Come. Would you like to see them? Those displays are not open to the public, but I think this collection will greatly intrigue such learned individuals as yourselves." He checked his watch. "We have a few minutes. Then we'll see the medallion. It truly is extraordinary."

They followed him up a wide marble staircase. The second floor was lined with windows overlooking a courtyard. A large tree with elliptical yellow-green leaves and a rounded crown nearly filled the space. A man wearing what looked like a beekeeper's outfit pruned branches, then put them in a wheelbarrow. A small apple rolled towards the edge of a boardwalk encircling the tree, and the man raced towards it before it could land in the surrounding soil. He picked it up with gloved hands, deposited it in the wheelbarrow, then looked up and saw the group of people watching him. The man frowned through the clear shield covering his face, then turned his back to them and resumed pruning.

Dr. Baker gave them a nervous smile. "That's Simon. He's a bit of an introvert, I suppose you'd say, but I've asked him to join us when we view the medallion exhibit. He's taken a keen interest in the project, which excites me as he's only ever cared about his plants, although that, too, I suppose is my fault." He paused, then rattled his head. "Shall we?" Dr. Baker gestured towards the glass cases embedded in alcoves, which shielded them from the sun pouring through the windows surrounding the courtyard.

Alex pulled out her phone to take pictures, but Dr. Baker moved to block her view of the closest case, shaking his head vigorously.

He spoke sternly. "Please, Ms. Paige, these displays are only for our members and donors. Photographs are strictly forbidden. We simply cannot present any of these items to the public, and I did not invite you here for that purpose."

"Oh!" she said, surprised at his vehemence. "My apologies. I'm so used to photographing and writing about everything I see, I just assumed—"

"Yes, yes, you know what they say about assuming, I presume? Well then, let's continue, but I expect you to respect that this is a *private* tour." He turned on his heel and strode quickly to the next case.

Alex slowly put her phone in the front pocket of her bag. She stood still, watching as the strange man moved to the next display case, pointing out items to Reid, who listened intently with his hands clasped behind his back.

"LuEllen never told me you two were a couple of trouble makers. Touching rare frames, photographing cursed artifacts. Tsk tsk tsk," Cassidy said with a wink.

"It seems inefficient to have an entire floor of a museum dedicated to displays that only a few people will see," Alex said. The three followed several feet behind the doctor and Reid. The display cases contained items from all over the world. She wished she had more time to examine them. Maybe she'd be able to come back later. *And maybe,* she thought ruefully, *William is right and I don't know how to take a vacation.*

"Exclusivity, my dear," William replied. "I bet museum membership is a hefty price, and they're able to get it because only the rarified few have access to this floor."

Cassidy nodded. "That's exactly right. This collection is legendary in certain circles, especially considering at least one patron inevitably dies after their big annual fundraiser."

"I imagine their donors are a bunch of old fogies, right?" William asked.

"Generally speaking, which is the explanation Reid and I believe. There are no curses, just old age."

"And the medallion? You seemed to have some questions about it, and its provenance," Alex said.

Before Cassidy could respond, they'd reached Reid and Dr. Baker, who had completed their circuit around the building and were waiting for them. "Fascinating," Reid said. "Cass, we might consider becoming members simply to have more time studying these finds."

Dr. Baker raised his eyebrows. "Oh, well, our memberships are quite, um, exclusive, but I'm certain we can provide information before you leave. Now, then, shall we go see Dr. Sterling's and Dr. Price's incredible find?" He started down the stairs without waiting for their answer.

"*Our memberships are quite exclusive*," Cassidy mimicked as she passed Alex to follow Dr. Baker. Alex could practically hear her teeth grinding.

Reid leaned in and spoke in Cassidy's ear, his voice a low murmur. Alex strained to listen. "He knows. But don't worry. We'll expose him again. We'll expose them all." Every muscle in Alex's body wanted to stop where she was, but if she did, it would be obvious she'd overheard him. William opened his mouth to speak, but Alex shook her head and mouthed, "Later." He acknowledged her with a miniscule tip of his head.

They reached the bottom of the stairs and turned right. Dr. Baker consulted his watch, then adjusted his glasses. "This way, please. I'm afraid we won't have much time." He opened a door marked Private. Alex glimpsed the lush courtyard she'd seen through the windows above. "Simon, join us. It's time."

Alex heard a grunt. "Fine. One moment." The man, wearing what Alex now realized was a hazmat suit, entered the hallway. Dr. Baker closed the door and tapped his foot while Simon removed his protective gear and deposited it in a wicker basket marked *Hazardous - Do Not Touch*.

"That doesn't seem like it would be very protective," William said, indicating the porous material.

"It's not meant to be. It's merely a deterrent to keep anyone from touching what's inside. It seems to work. So far." Simon adjusted wire-rimmed glasses perched on the end of his nose. He tugged at the hem of his olive green polo and walked briskly to the front of the group. The keys attached to his belt clanged, and his khaki pants whisked as his legs brushed each other.

"What in the world are they growing in there?" William asked, pausing to look at the closed door.

"I recognized that tree in the center," Alex said. "It's a manchineel."

"A what?"

"*La manzanilla de la muerte*. The little apple of death," Reid answered. "Also deceivingly known as the beach apple."

"Why in the world would anyone intentionally grow something like that?"

"Because it's native to Florida, Mexico, and the Caribbean, and Indians murdered Spaniards with its poison, including Juan Ponce de León," Simon snapped. "It's also the *curse* part of many of the cursed items we display. We tell the story of the explorers, and weapons are part of it." He pulled the ring of keys, stretching the coiled cord that attached it to his belt, and opened a set of thick cedar doors to the Beauregard Chalmers Exhibition Hall.

"Murdered?" Cassidy sneered. "They were defending their homes."

Simon waved his hand. "Whatever."

Cassidy clenched her fists. Reid put his hand on her back. While the dynamic between Vanessa and Gerald had seemed like one of conflict, Alex felt this couple had a more symbiotic relationship. She'd only met them the night before, but had already witnessed their unspoken communications multiple times, and they were usually met with a return to some sort of baseline. Cassidy was definitely the hothead of the two.

Dr. Baker stepped to the side and encouraged the group to enter the darkly lit room. Recessed lights reflected off the chrome edges of glass cases lined up against the wall. The main attraction stood in the center, surrounded by velvet ropes. Cassidy barreled towards the display. She moved the stanchion and peered through the glass at the medallion.

"Hey, you can't—" Simon began, lurching towards the intent woman.

Dr. Baker grabbed his arm. "No, no, it's fine. They're experts. I want them to verify for themselves the authenticity of this remarkable discovery." He released Simon, then reached into a cabinet below the case and extracted a box of archivist's gloves. He nodded at the younger man. "Please unlock the case. I'd like them to get a closer look."

"Father," Simon reprimanded. "I do not think that is a good idea."

Alex looked back and forth between the two men. Their similarities stopped at the wire-rimmed glasses. Where Dr. Baker was short, slightly pudgy, and seemed to constantly be in motion, Simon was tall and lanky. There was a stiffness about him. Alex couldn't tell if it was because he disagreed with his father, or if that was simply the way he moved. William raised his eyebrows at her. She could tell her friend wanted to say something, but his whispers were notoriously loud, and for once, he wisely decided against it.

Reid eyed the younger Baker. "So, the museum is a family affair. I had heard rumors the prodigal son had returned. It must be an experience to work so closely with your father, especially considering his reputation. We've heard stories about his career for years."

Simon glared, then shifted his gaze to Dr. Baker. "It's definitely an experience," he grunted. "You're sure?" he asked. When his father nodded confirmation, he grabbed a pair of gloves before walking to the case and bending over. He opened the cover of a keypad and entered a long code, shielding his action with his other hand. After a series of beeps, a hiss escaped from the case. Simon gently eased the panel open, then reached in and extracted the medallion from its platform.

Cassidy and Reid donned gloves as well. She held out her hands. Simon hesitated. "You must be very, very careful with this. It's priceless," he said.

"Don't worry, son," Dr. Baker said, shifting from one foot to the other, drumming his fingers against his thighs. "As I said, they're experts. They know how to handle antiquities."

"Besides," William said. "It's been buried for centuries, right? It can handle a little handling."

Cassidy shook her head, her eyes focused on the medallion. "No. The earth protects it. Once an item is excavated and exposed to the elements, it's in much more danger. That's why museums display them with special lighting and within vitrines." William raised his eyebrows. Cassidy didn't remove her attention from the artifact, but she seemed to sense his confusion. "Museum quality glass cases," she explained.

Alex leaned in to get a closer look. Even though she'd seen the photo of it on Dr. Baker's invitation, the image had been small and didn't capture the artifact's beauty. She estimated its size at about three inches in diameter, large enough to capture attention, yet small enough to be worn as a pendant. Alex pictured the ancient queen, her skin bronzed from years in the sun, the medallion strung through a leather strap and resting on her chest. As Cassidy tilted the artifact, light reflected from its surface. Braided and coiled strands of gold created an elaborate and delicate setting. A cougar's face, inlaid with eyes of pearl, seemed to leap forward, its incisors slightly bared. Alex looked from the medallion to Cassidy and back again.

Cassidy raised her eyes to Reid, then handed him the medallion. He examined it closely, then turned it over. Cassidy leaned in close enough their temples touched. Without looking, she reached into a small bag at her waist and pulled out a jeweler's loupe.

"Seriously?" Simon said. "You can't do that. They can't do that."

"Simon," warned Dr. Baker, "I invited them here precisely so they *would* do that. I know you've had questions about the authenticity of this find," he said to the archaeologists. "I invite you to inspect as much as you need to confirm its veracity." The bumbling professor act had completely disappeared. He consulted his watch again. "I have much to do before tomorrow's opening. Simon, please stay with them and return this priceless treasure to the case when they are finished."

Dr. Baker brushed past Alex without a word. Simon frowned and watched him exit, then turned to Cassidy. "You heard him. Take your time. Except don't take too much time. I also have more important things to do than babysit you while you waste ours. The artifact is real. My father verified it himself."

"Exactly," Cassidy muttered. She tilted the medallion in Reid's hand and leaned closer, her loupe practically touching one of the pearls.

"Careful!" Simon warned.

"Shhh," she said. She straightened up, then replaced the magnifying glass in her bag and focused on Reid. Her lips parted slightly, exposing a glimpse of her teeth. Without a word, she spun around and walked towards the door.

"Wait," Simon commanded. "Where are you going?"

She ignored him, rushing to the end of the corridor. She turned in the same direction Dr. Baker had taken.

"To find your father," Reid said. "The medallion is a fake."

Chapter 5

Simon exploded. "That is not possible. It *can't* be. He *promised* it was real," he whined, panic crossing his features. He started for the hallway, then returned to Reid and thrust his hand out. "Give me the medallion." Reid complied. Simon examined it, turning it in multiple directions. "Looks real enough to me," he muttered, before putting it back in the case. The panel snicked shut. He stared at the artifact, now returned safely to its platform. He chewed on his lip, then started for the door, whipping his hand at them. "Follow me. All of you."

They entered the hallway right as Cassidy raced around the corner at the opposite end, hurrying towards them with her phone to her ear. "Yes, the archaeology museum. Hurry. *You must hurry.*" She passed Reid, grasping his hand briefly, and stopped in front of Simon. "I need you to come with me."

"Why?"

"Just, please, just come with me," her voice softened. "It's your father. Something... something's happened."

Simon looked at her with alarm, then pushed past her. The group followed as he raced down the hall, turned the corner, and yanked open a door at the end of the corridor. It began closing behind him, but Cassidy caught it and held it open for the rest. Before they were close enough to see inside, Simon screamed.

"No! Father! No!" he cried. Alex entered the room behind Reid and saw Simon standing in front of his father. Dr. Baker lay on the floor, his lifeless hands clutching his throat. He lay in a pool of viscous liquid in front of a monstrous mahogany desk, a shattered mug near his right hand, his fingers still looped around the handle. Simon bent over to sniff the liquid. He reared back, covering his mouth and looking around frantically, his eyes settling on Cassidy. "You!" he shouted. "You did this! You killed him!"

Cassidy's eyes opened wide. She began to protest, but sirens cut her off. She gave Reid a pleading look and he exited the room. Alex watched as he ran, pivoting around the corner. The sirens stopped. "Simon, your father was like this when I came in," Cassidy said. "I called 911 as soon as I saw him."

"Liar," he shrieked. "I know what you think of him, and how you feel about his life's work. Oh, yes, I know all about you and your, your vendetta."

Vendetta? Alex wondered. She heard voices, which grew louder as they neared Dr. Baker's office. A wall of windows provided a view of the interior courtyard, with its shapely, and deadly, tree.

A stocky woman with wildly curly black hair tamed into a ponytail barged into the office and stopped, her hand resting on the gun at her hip. She focused on the body on the floor, then nodded at the tall man behind her. He moved around her and walked towards Dr. Baker. The woman turned to face Simon, who'd moved behind the desk and was pacing stiffly back and forth. Alex and William shuffled as far out of the way as they could, standing against a back wall lined with bookshelves.

The woman spoke. "I'm Detective Elsie Monroe and this is Detective Darrell Washington," she said, then moved aside to allow two paramedics to enter the room. "Simon, we came as quickly as we could."

"I'll say. What, were they waiting outside?" William attempted to say under his breath.

Detective Monroe glared at him, but didn't respond. Instead, she motioned the paramedics towards the body. One of the young men kneeled next to Dr. Baker and reached for him. Simon ran around the desk, clipping the corner and knocking off a pile of loose papers precariously balanced on the edge. They fluttered to the floor, landing near Alex's feet. She ignored them and focused on Simon, who was grabbing the medic's wrist. "Stop!" he commanded. "You can't touch him."

Everyone's attention was focused on the two men, and Alex knelt, picking up the papers. It looked like they were out of order after their fall, but she didn't think it would be a good idea to arrange them. Instead, she stacked them neatly and placed them back on the desk. Something on the top sheet caught her attention. She did a double take, then snuck her phone out of her pocket and acted like she was reading a text. William noticed. He raised an eyebrow at her and she moved her head subtly back and forth.

The medic wrenched his arm free. With his tousled hair and deep tan, he looked like he'd come straight from surfing. He leaned towards the body. Simon tried to pull him back by his shoulder, but the young man held. "You can't touch him," Simon repeated.

Detective Washington spoke. "Mr. Baker," he said, the deep rumble of his voice sounding a warning. "I realize this is difficult, but you must let him do his job."

Simon shook his head. "No, you don't understand. That," he said, pointing to the spilled liquid, "is one of the deadliest poisons known to man. If you touch it, if you even breathe too much of it, you could get blisters on your skin and in your throat." Simon coughed and covered his mouth with this hand.

The EMTs arrested their movements and slowly backed up. Detective Washington squinted at Simon, then took in the rest of the room. William and Alex pushed themselves further against the bookshelves, trying to stay out of the way.

Detective Monroe followed her partner's action, looking from person to person. Although Dr. Baker's office was large, large enough to fit a gargantuan desk, multiple bookshelves, a mammoth globe, and a seating area that faced the courtyard, the number of people made it seem crowded. Alex and William huddled in the corner. Cassidy and Reid stood on the opposite side next to the open door, nearly hidden by the sun streaming through the windows. Dust motes floated like fizzled-out fireflies. Simon resumed pacing, running his fingers through his hair and making it stand on end. The paramedics waited for instructions from the two detectives, who flanked them. From her vantage point in the back of the room, Alex thought it seemed like the sort of tableau you'd see on a grim Norman Rockwell painting, or maybe a murder mystery. She half expected Monk or Jessica Fletcher to swoop in at any moment.

The detective's sweeping gaze froze on Cassidy. Her eyes widened, then narrowed as she seemed to recognize the lithe blonde. "What are you doing here?" she hissed.

Cassidy exhaled, a long breath that spoke volumes. "Hello, Elsie. It's been awhile. I almost didn't recognize you."

"That's Detective Monroe to you. I repeat: what are you doing here? Aren't you supposed to be off in Guatemala or something?" Her nose wrinkled in distaste.

"Nice of you to keep track of me, Detective Monroe. LuEllen's opening was last night, as I'm sure you know, since I believe a few of your colleagues were there."

"Yes, of course. Everybody knew about your sister's opening. Although, I'm surprised you could take time away from your globetrotting to support her." Detective Monroe's partner cleared his throat. She closed her eyes, then refocused on Cassidy. "But why are you *here*?" the detective asked, jabbing her index finger toward the floor.

"I could ask the same of you. I thought patrol officers arrived first. Seems like Dr. Baker warrants special treatment. Typical," Cassidy snorted.

Reid gave her a quelling look, then spoke to the detective. "To answer your question, we met Dr. Baker last night at LuEllen's opening and he invited us to get an early look at the new exhibit."

"From what I heard, you invited yourselves," Simon sputtered. "Stop! Get back!" he shouted at Detective Washington. The other officer had been circling Dr. Baker's body, getting dangerously close as he knelt to get a better look. At Simon's command, he froze, his knee inches from the spreading pool of liquid. "You need to move away from that very, very carefully," Simon warned. "Weren't you listening? If *any* of that gets on you, it will cause burning and blisters. It could be fatal. And I promise you, that is a horrible way to die." He looked sadly at his father, whose eyes were permanently frozen in pain. "I'm sorry," he whispered.

Detective Monroe spoke gently. "Simon, what exactly are you apologizing for?"

Simon closed his eyes, squeezed them tight, then opened them. "It's my fault. He created this garden so I'd come home," he said, gesturing to the verdant courtyard beyond the glass. Alex followed his arm. Through the window she recognized at least three other deadly plants.

"Is that spotted water hemlock?" William whispered.

"Yes," Simon answered. "And foxglove and oleander, among other less lethal specimens. I've made it my life's work to study these evolutionary paradoxes. Father knew I couldn't resist the opportunity to work with them, hands on, that this would bring me here." Simon slumped, burying his face in his hands. "Why, Father? Why did you drink it? Couldn't you smell what it was?"

His father didn't answer.

Simon lifted his gaze towards the courtyard, the late morning sun beating down on the lethal tree and washing out its yellow-green leaves. Alex followed his eyes toward the wheelbarrow. Filled with trimmed branches still bearing fruit, it seemed almost within reach. Simon turned away from the garden, then raised his hand and pointed at Cassidy. "Are you happy now?" he seethed.

Detective Monroe raised her hands to stop him. "Simon, I'll take care of this." She looked around the room. "Obviously, we'll need to speak to all of you. Especially you," she said, glaring at Cassidy, then turned back to Simon. "Is there someplace we can talk? Your office perhaps?"

Simon tugged at his collar, stretched his neck, and tore his stare from Cassidy. "Yes, of course. We have a boardroom upstairs." He then spoke to the paramedics, who were still waiting silently. "Do you have protective gear? Good. I suggest you get it." The medics waited for confirmation from Detective Monroe, then left the room.

Her partner cleared his throat. "Mr. Baker, you seem awfully positive about the cause of death. Is there a reason for that?"

Detective Monroe frowned, but Simon answered, sadness lacing his words. "I've seen what happens when someone ingests anything from the manchineel. That," he said, waving to his father's body, "is what it looks like, and that liquid is what it smells like." He took one last look at the contorted figure, then silently walked past them all towards the hallway.

Monroe's radio crackled. She listened, then spoke to her partner. "That's CID. They're on their way. I'll stay here until they arrive." She turned to Cassidy. "You—all of you—follow Mr. Baker and Detective Washington."

Cassidy gave Dr. Baker one last look, then filed out with Reid, ignoring Detective Monroe. Cassidy wrapped her arms around her body and studied her feet as she walked. Reid matched her pace, walking close to her, but not touching. William followed them. He paused and turned to look at Alex, who stood with her head down, frozen.

Detective Monroe spoke. "Time to move along, Ms...."

"Paige. Alex Paige." Alex took a sweeping look around the room, noticing multiple diplomas. Photos of Dr. Baker shaking hands with dignitaries, including one that looked like a much younger Dr. Sterling, flanked a framed yellowed map that detailed the Spaniards' marches across the New World. "Sorry, Detective," she said, then moved to follow the rest.

"It's fine. I know this had to be a shock. Most people don't know how to react when they see a dead person," she said, much more kindly than she'd spoken to Cassidy.

Alex stopped with her back to the room, then simply nodded. She didn't think it would be a good idea to tell a police officer, especially at the scene of a murder, this wasn't her first dead person. It wasn't even her third.

Chapter 6

"I. Did. Not. Kill. Him!"

The words pierced through the closed door to the reception area outside the boardroom. Reid completed multiple circuits around the room, prowling like a jungle cat waiting to pounce as Cassidy's protestations increased in volume.

"Cassidy Devereaux, sit down or I will arrest you right here and now!" Detective Monroe shouted.

Reid stopped in front of the door and raised his fist to knock. Detective Washington shook his head. "Shouldn't you be in there with her?" Reid asked. "Why is Cass even talking to her? She knows better than that," he growled.

The door slammed open, nearly hitting Reid. Cassidy stormed into the middle of the room, then spun around. "Do it. Arrest me, Elsie. Let's make all your dreams come true." She thrust her arms out, wrists touching.

Detective Monroe appeared in the doorway, her cheeks flushed and eyes blazing. "Elsie," Detective Washington warned.

Monroe shifted her glare from Cassidy and directed it at her partner. She slowly calmed, taking deeper breaths, then straightened her spine and looked around the room. "Why are you all still here?" she hissed. "I told you, each one of you, you could leave."

"Trauma," Reid explained. "We've experienced a collective trauma. It's safer to stay together. At least, that's what our lizard brains tell us."

Monroe rolled her eyes. "Bunch of mumbo-jumbo. Go. All of you. We *will* have more questions, so do not leave town." She focused on Simon. "Your father was a great man, and I will find out who murdered him," she promised. The detectives left the room, walking rapidly.

The group followed Simon out of the reception area to the hallway. Alex approached him slowly. "I'm sorry for your loss," she said, looking through the windows and down at the courtyard as she walked next to him.

He stopped, facing the tree whose poison had killed his father. "I don't understand. Why would he drink it? He had to have known what it was."

"Forgive me for saying so, but what if he didn't?" Alex asked. Simon frowned, without turning his head. She continued. "Are you positive he would know what it smelled like? In the cup, it probably looked like coffee."

The botanist's shoulders slumped. "Maybe you're right. I expected him to know, because I know."

"Were you close?" Alex asked. Through her peripheral vision, she saw William approach. She turned slightly towards Simon and William took the hint, walking by with Cassidy and Reid.

Simon choked a short laugh. "I don't think you'd say we were close, no. We saw things...differently, I suppose you'd say." He paused, then seemed to steel himself, straightening his spine and pushing his glasses up, just like Alex had seen his father do multiple times. "Thank you for your kindness."

Alex nodded. "I suppose the exhibit's opening will be canceled."

"Absolutely not," he said with surprising force, facing her. "This was Father's dream. His redemption. I must continue. It's what he would have wanted." He began walking towards the stairs. "Come. I'm sure your friends are waiting for you, and I have much to do."

She followed him silently. As they reached the first floor, she heard the detectives talking and figured they were heading back to Dr. Baker's office. Simon opened the heavy entrance doors and the sun blinded Alex. She lightly squeezed his shoulder as she passed him. He bristled, then stepped back. "I will see you tomorrow," Simon stated, then spoke to William, Cassidy, and Reid, who waited on the sidewalk leading up to the museum's entrance. "I will see you all tomorrow."

The door closed with a muffled thud.

William buried his toes in the sand. "Who grows spotted water hemlock? That stuff'll practically kill you just from looking at it. You'd have to be some kind of sociopath."

"Or a dedicated scientist, someone interested in the pathology of such dangerous organisms."

"How you can still be such a Pollyanna after everything you've seen is beyond me."

Alex shrugged. "It's how I stay sane."

"Who said you were sane?" he winked. Alex laughed, then reached down to retrieve a can of flavored San Pellegrino from the cooler sitting between them. They'd parted from Cassidy and Reid when they left the museum and had driven to William's campsite at Gulf State Park. Although it was across a four-lane road from the beach, there was still sand everywhere, interspersed with shrub grass and oak trees. A canopy extended from Bessie's roof provided shade from the early afternoon sun.

"I will say that was one of the easiest police interviews I've done," she said.

"Easy for us. Not so much for Cassidy," he said. "But the fact that you can say that—that *we* can say that—causes me a bit of concern, my dear. Before I met you, I was not the kind of person who was regularly interviewed by the police."

"Unless it's *your* police," Alex teased. "Did you need to call Billy? Let him know what's going on?"

"I texted him. His reply was, 'of course,' followed immediately by an offer to come down and straighten out this Detective Monroe person. I declined."

"Everything OK with you two?"

"Fine. It's fine." He caught her suspicious look. "No, really. We're good. It's just also good to be alone."

"I hear you on that one." She drained the can and crossed the small campsite to throw it away inside Bessie. William had placed a blue recycle bin right inside the steps, which he secured behind teak cabinets when he was on the road. "OK if we go for a walk? I need to move."

"Certainly," William said, extracting himself from the folding camp chair. An ingress to the trail system began at the end of the cul-de-sac where he'd set up camp. They reached the boardwalk that protected hikers and bikers from the undergrowth, walking slowly. "I detect a bit of a conflict within," he said.

Alex sighed. "That was awful. Simply awful. To see him like that. What a terrible, terrible way to die."

"Do you think Cassidy did it?"

"No. Why would she? Frankly, how could she? She didn't have time, did she? Or access?" Alex stopped, then looked at him with suspicion. "I see what you're doing."

"Whatever do you mean?" he asked, batting his eyes.

"Stop it," she said, lightly punching him in the arm. "You're trying to get me to investigate this, aren't you?"

"Maybe," William said, drawing the word out.

"No. Absolutely not. I haven't had to try to figure out who killed someone in months and I'd like to keep it that way. What happened to Dr. Baker is sad, but Monroe and Washington seem competent. Well, at least Washington does. I'm sure they've got it under control."

"Um hmm. Sure. But what about LuEllen?"

"What about LuEllen?"

"On your left," a voice called from behind. William moved over to follow Alex single-file and let a cyclist pass them. The tires rumbled and clicked on the boardwalk like a train.

"Didn't it seem like she had the hots for dear old Harold?" William said, pulling up alongside Alex again. "She's going to be upset when she hears about his death."

She shook her head. "Even if she did and she is, it's still none of my business."

William gasped with mock horror. "Who are you and what have you done with my friend?"

Alex sighed. "Someone who's craving some semblance of normalcy." She stopped and rested her arms on the railing of the boardwalk. A slight breeze ruffled the foliage and blew strands of hair into her face. She smiled. *I missed that feeling*, she thought, relishing how quickly her hair was growing back after months of baldness.

The friends were silent for a moment, Alex lost in the memories of her year of treatment, followed by back-to-back murders. The last few months, a relatively drama-free period of travel and work, and no unexpected deaths, had given her hope that life was returning to normal. Although, she was beginning to realize, there was no such thing as normal.

William squeezed her hand. He didn't speak. That trait of his, the ability to know when to stop talking and let someone be, was one of the reasons Alex loved him. They turned around to walk back to the campsite. "I can't believe Simon's still going through with the opening tomorrow night. Seems rather heartless," he said.

"Especially after Cassidy dropped the bomb about the medallion. I wonder why she thinks it's a fake?"

"I don't think she *thinks* it's a fake. I'd say she *knows* it's a fake. She seemed dead–" William blanched. "Poor choice of words; sorry. She was certain it's a fake, and Reid agreed with her."

"True, but they also obviously have a past with Vanessa and Gerald. I have a feeling they'd call into question anything the doctors claimed to discover." Alex heard rustling and stopped, looking over the railing. "Look! An armadillo! I've never seen one of those in the wild."

"It's so cute," William cooed. "Who would've thought a creature coated in armor could be cute? Anyway," he continued, resuming their trek back to the campground, "it sounds like you don't believe them either."

Alex shrugged. "I have a feeling about them."

"Those spidey senses again. Did you see Dr. Baker had an entire shelf devoted to books by Dr. Vanessa Sterling?"

She nodded. "Whatever Cassidy thinks of her, she was prolific, and the doctor was certainly a fan. Even had a framed photo of her on his wall."

"Maybe we should find out more about those two," William prompted. "If we're going to the opening, a little background info on the doctors wouldn't hurt. And who knows what else we'll discover," he said with a wink.

Alex narrowed her eyes at him, but her grin proved she wasn't upset. She knew, as an innate gossip, he couldn't resist a good mystery. Truth be told, neither could she. It's what had made her a good investigative journalist, and why her travel stories were filled with insights others often missed. An example of that curiosity was the photo on her phone from Dr. Baker's office. Alex didn't know what had prompted her to snap the picture of the paper, especially if she was as determined as she claimed to be to resist getting involved. *Actually*, she thought ruefully, *you know exactly what prompted it.* "I know what you're doing, William Meriwether Blake, and I am not going to get roped into investigating Dr. Baker's death. End of story."

"Of course," he winked. "Whatever you say."

They reached the end of the boardwalk. As they neared Bessie, they could see LuEllen pacing frantically in front of the decked-out van. "There you are!" she cried, then raced to them. "Oh, thank heavens you're back." She grabbed Alex by the shoulders. "Elsie arrested Cassidy! You have to help her. You just have to."

"Elsie?" William asked.

"*Detective* Monroe," LuEllen spat. "Please, Cassidy didn't kill Harold. I know she didn't, but that, that *woman* will do whatever it takes to punish my Cass."

End of story, eh? Famous last words, Alex thought, then shook it off. She led LuEllen to the chairs circling the campsite's fire ring. LuEllen sat down, wringing her hands and rocking. Alex leaned forward and grasped one of them, gently caressing the skin wrinkled from decades in the southern sun. LuEllen's breathing slowed and she extracted her hand, pulling a tissue from under her waistband, then noisily blowing her nose and wiping the tears from her eyes. William popped open a can of sparkling water and handed it to her. She took a sip, and nodded, as if to herself.

"Better?" Alex asked.

LuEllen raised haunted eyes to her. "I warned her not to get involved," she said, "but Cassidy can't see straight when it comes to anything related to the conquistadors, or to those supposed doctors," she said with disdain. "I told Cass she didn't need to inspect the medallion. It's not her responsibility. But would she listen? No. She's always been more headstrong than a shark in a pool full of chum. I barely survived her teens. So did she, come to think of it."

"We left the museum at the same time as Cassidy and Reid. If we'd had any idea she'd be arrested, we would have stayed with them," William said, as he took the chair on LuEllen's other side.

LuEllen rattled her head, her white curls shaking. "It wouldn't have mattered. Elsie's been looking for a way to get back at Cass for decades."

Alex and William eyed each other over LuEllen's head, both raising their eyebrows. "Tell us exactly what happened," Alex said, realizing she would do whatever it took to prove Cassidy's innocence. William nodded, and she knew he would be right there with her.

Chapter 7

LuEllen crumpled the soiled tissue, repeatedly squeezing it and smoothing it out. Alex didn't know LuEllen well, but she knew this was distinctly uncharacteristic. The older woman always seemed like she was in charge, like she could handle anything. But Alex also knew she had raised Cassidy like she was her daughter instead of her sister. After their parents had died in a horrible car crash, LuEllen left her career as an engineer in Baton Rouge, moved back to Alabama, and took on the role of her five-year-old sister's guardian. It couldn't have been easy, Alex mused.

"They came to the new Shack to tell me about Harold," LuEllen began. "Cassidy and Reid, I mean. I was just getting to know him," she said sadly. The tissue had practically disintegrated, and she put it back in her pocket.

"That surprises me," William said. "Weren't both of you from here?"

LuEllen shrugged, and when she spoke, it was with undeniable mourning. "This place isn't as small as you think, young man. Plus, I've spent most of my days, and nights, at work. It's why Cassidy's teen years were so hard. After mom and dad died, I had to work constantly to support us, so I was never home. I spent nearly every waking moment at my uncle's restaurant." She paused and gazed into the past. Alex remembered LuEllen had had a similar reaction when she'd mentioned him in Colorado.

The older woman met Alex's eyes. She took a deep breath. When she spoke again, her voice was stronger. "And then I went out on my own. No time for museum visits for me. I'd heard of Dr. Baker, of course. Everyone 'round here knew about his 'exclusive' second-floor exhibits. Oh, the stories people would tell. They'd get a glimpse of those oddities and then come into the Shack and see poison everywhere." She chuckled lightly. "Sounds terrible for a restaurant, but I made a game of it. Started naming dishes "Curse of the Bottom Feeders," that kind of thing. Took a while, but he finally got wind of it. I met him last month when I catered his big fundraiser. What a to-do that was," she paused. "Such a funny little man."

Alex and William waited. They both knew not to prompt her. LuEllen took a shaky breath. "I went to the docks this morning, like I do every day, and when I got back I was planning tonight's specials when Cass and Reid burst into my office, practically knocking down my poor assistant. That toothpick couldn't stop those two if he tried. That's when they told me." LuEllen clasped her hands, rubbing her thumbs against each other. Alex was afraid if she rubbed any harder, she'd start a fire.

"After that news, well, I needed some fresh air, so we walked out front. First thing I noticed was they'd parked all catty wampus."

"Is that odd?" Alex asked.

LuEllen nodded. "Couple of perfectionists, those two. Seeing that? I knew something was very, very wrong. Besides Harold being murdered, of course." She blushed.

"Surely that would have been enough," William said.

"You don't know my sister." LuEllen looked at her watch and began to stand. She'd calmed down considerably and seemed more like her usual take-charge self. "What're we doing, sitting here chatting like a hen circle? I'll explain on the way."

Alex and William exchanged a glance, then got up and followed the determined woman. Alex got into the front seat of LuEllen's convertible Beetle. It was an early body type; Alex guessed it dated back to the early sixties. Despite its age, it looked to be in pristine condition.

"Well, she's a beaut," William said. Instead of getting in, he closed the door and held his hand out. Alex handed him her keys and he walked to her car, eyeing the powder blue classic the entire way.

"Isn't he coming?" LuEllen asked, the panic in her voice returning.

"He's going to follow us," Alex soothed.

"OK, OK, that makes sense," she said, nodding to herself, her white curls bouncing. "In case you have to leave or go somewhere else." She pursed her lips. "I don't know what's come over me. I'm normally not this flighty."

"Maybe because someone you cared for is gone, and because your sister is being blamed? Give yourself a little grace," Alex comforted.

LuEllen closed her eyes. She breathed deeply and tilted her head back, then opened them and peered through her windshield with determination. Alex winced as gears ground and the Beetle lurched forward. "Sorry," she said. "I don't have cause to drive much around here. Betty stays in the garage most of the time."

Betty? Alex suppressed a grin, knowing it was entirely inappropriate. William had Bessie; LuEllen had Betty. Did Alex need to name her Subaru Barney? Bertha? Beatrice? She shook her head to focus on what LuEllen was saying.

"Now where was I? Oh, yes. We went out front," LuEllen said, back to explaining what happened when Cassidy and Reid had given her the news about Harold. "I needed some fresh air, see, and I couldn't handle dealing with any customers." They reached the exit to the campground and LuEllen pulled onto State Route 182, screeching tires as she turned. The light was already yellow, so William raced through to keep up with them, earning a few angry horns. "I was just starting to pull myself together when that darn Elsie pulled up. Fool woman jumped out of her unmarked and yelled at Cass like she was some sort of criminal."

LuEllen blasted through another yellow light and Alex gripped the dashboard. She turned to see William stuck at the intersection. Alex's phone vibrated. *Google Maps is my friend*, she read. *See you at the station.*

"I tried to stop her, but she and that Washington fellow insisted Cass get in the car and go with them."

"Did they handcuff her?" Alex asked, although she was reluctant to do or say anything to distract LuEllen from driving. The woman was even more of a force in a vehicle than she was on two feet. A force Alex hoped would make it safely to where they were going.

"Yes. No. I don't know, I can't remember," LuEllen said, shaking her head and closing her eyes.

"Hey, LuEllen, could you please, maybe, open your eyes?" It amazed Alex at how calm her voice sounded as they rapidly approached a bus full of tourists.

LuEllen did, then slammed on the brakes. She turned to Alex. "She took her. Elsie put my baby sister in the back of her car and took her." The car behind them laid on the horn and LuEllen flipped him the bird before accelerating.

"And Reid?"

"He followed her. At least, I assume he did." They made another rapid turn, complete with screeching tires, and pulled into a parking lot filled with police cars. "Yep, he did. That's theirs," LuEllen said, pointing to a bright blue Ford F150. The vehicle seemed like an odd choice for the couple until Alex realized it was an electric truck. The front door of the police station opened and Cassidy emerged, followed closely by Reid. LuEllen pulled in next to the large pickup and she jumped out before coming to a complete stop. Alex pried her fingers out of the dashboard. As she stood up, LuEllen shouted. "Cass! Cass! That dirty little piece of too big for her britches worn-out shoe leather let you go?" she asked, racing to her sister.

Cassidy braced herself as LuEllen plowed into her and wrapped her in a tight hug. Reid stood to the side. He lifted his eyes and Alex turned to see what had gotten his attention. William was pulling into the lot, much more calmly than LuEllen had.

William slowly got out of Alex's SUV and walked over to her. He began patting her shoulders and back, then turned her hands over and counted her fingers.

"What are you doing?" she asked.

"Making sure you're still in one piece. Remind me never to get in a car when that one's driving," he said, pointing to LuEllen, who was still embracing Cassidy.

"I don't think you'll need much reminding. I certainly won't." Alex shook herself off, then walked over to the three people huddled together on the sidewalk. Reid caught her eyes in the glass door's reflection.

"Lu, Lu, I'm fine. Please. I can't breathe," Cassidy complained. LuEllen finally released her, then patted her sister, unconsciously repeating William's movements.

"You're OK? Evil Elsie let you go?"

Cassidy took a deep breath. "Please, do not call her that. She was just doing her job."

"Didn't look like it to me. Looked like she was arresting you."

"She just wanted to ask me more questions."

"Well, why'd she have to haul you in like some kind of felon? Why on God's green earth couldn't she have asked you questions at the Shack?"

"Because then she would have been shackled?" William whispered. Reid burst out laughing.

Cassidy smiled and shook her head at him, then turned back to her sister. "Why don't we go somewhere else and talk." She looked over LuEllen's head at Alex. "Thanks for coming with her, especially in Betty. I'm sure that was one heck of a ride. I know how she drives," she winked. "C'mon, Lu. Let's go to your place and have some of that lovely sweet tea."

Alex and William headed towards the Subaru. "Wait!" LuEllen cried. "Y'all are coming with us, right?"

Reid frowned. "I'm sure they have things they need to do, don't you?" he asked them.

William vigorously shook his head. "Not me," he said, a bit too cheerfully for Alex's taste. "This morning wiped our calendars clean, didn't it, Miss Marple?"

Alex slumped. She ignored the looks of confusion on Reid's and Cassidy's faces. "Fine. But can I get the address? I am not riding in that thing again," she said, pointing at the Volkswagen.

The three vehicles pulled out of the police station's parking lot like a caravan, one led by a powder blue streak that took off and quickly disappeared. Although Alex had the address, she was glad Reid drove at a more reasonable speed and avoided racing through intersections as the lights switched to red. They turned north, then headed east and drove parallel to the Intracoastal Waterway. The narrow body of water made Alex think of the ancient canal she'd planned to see the next morning. She wondered if she'd get the chance.

Reid turned into a driveway made of shells and Alex pulled in behind him. LuEllen must have already gone inside. Alex neared the Beetle parked under the house between stilts. She could hear the knocking of the engine as it cooled. The house was the same powder blue as the convertible. White shutters and trim made it look like a gingerbread cottage. All it needed were a few gumdrops on the roof to complete the image. They climbed steep steps and, instead of entering the front door, Cassidy led them around the house towards the back.

"This is the most literal wraparound porch I've ever seen," William quipped. He gasped as they reached the back of the deck. Across an inlet, a break in the line of highrise condos revealed a stretch of sparkling sand and the Gulf beyond. "Now this is what I call a slice of heaven."

LuEllen backed out of the house, pushing the screen door open with her behind. She carried a tray with a pitcher filled with iced tea and colorful plastic tumblers. Reid walked over to relieve her of the refreshments, setting them on a large picnic table in the shade of the overhanging roof. The back porch extended beyond the awning. The areas in the sun were filled with pots of herbs, lettuce, and flowers. Alex rubbed some basil between her fingers and inhaled the distinctive scent before joining the group at the table. She took a deep breath, deciding that jumping in was the only way to go.

"So," she said, looking directly at Cassidy, "tell me about this vendetta."

Chapter 8

Cassidy tilted her head and gave Alex a narrow smile. "I'm surprised you remembered Simon said that."

"It's a memorable word, especially since it seemed so out of place," Alex explained.

"Plus, this one pays attention," William said, pointing his thumb at Alex, "so be careful what you say if she's around," he whispered dramatically.

Cassidy laughed. "Good to know."

"So?" Alex prompted. "What did he mean?"

Reid looked at Cassidy, and when she didn't answer, he spoke up. "It's not a vendetta. That's a very dramatic word. It's more..."

"Ancient history," Cassidy finished.

"Isn't that what you do?" William asked. "Ancient history's kind of your thing."

Cassidy looked at her sister. "You may not want to hear this, Lu."

LuEllen poured her version of sweet tea into a different color tumbler for each of them and passed them around. "Don't you decide what I want to hear. Spill it, Cass."

The younger sister's lips thinned, but when she spoke, it was with compassion. "I know you liked him," Cassidy said, "but he didn't deserve you." She raised her hand to stop LuEllen's objection. "Remember that thesis I wrote? The one that exposed a professor's fraud and the university subsequently fired him? That was Dr. Harold Baker."

William reached under the table and punched Alex's thigh. She winced, then coughed to cover it up.

LuEllen's face was immobile. "Explain."

Cassidy swallowed, and Alex could see the mother-daughter dynamic that superseded their relationship as sisters. "I heard about this professor who said he found what he called the 'Iberian Diadem.' What a ridiculous name," Cassidy scoffed. "He claimed it was from the 16th century, that it was a ceremonial crown used by the native tribes to welcome the Spanish explorers, that it symbolized the, quote unquote, peaceful transfer of power from the indigenous population to the Spaniards." She clenched her fists. Reid placed his hand on top of hers.

"It would have completely changed the narrative," Reid explained. "Instead of violent conquest, he claimed colonization was peaceful. Welcome, even."

"How could anyone believe this?" Alex asked.

"Because they wanted to," Cassidy said bitterly. "Generational guilt, I suppose? Or the belief that they really were saving the 'poor savages.' Either way, I did the research this professor should have, and found out the supposed relic dated not to the 16th century, but to the 19th."

"Fauxtiquities," Reid continued. "They were a big thing in the 1800s. Charlatans would manufacture these so-called antiquities for commercial gain. Cassidy's thesis proved the Diadem was made in the 1800s, not the 1500s. It ended up costing Dr. Baker his job."

"He cost himself his job," Cassidy defended hotly.

"He did indeed," Reid said.

"Is that when he moved down here?" William asked.

LuEllen nodded. "Must have been. I remember hearing about this new museum right when I opened my first place. I wanted to check it out, but never had the time."

"In twenty years?"

"You've obviously never worked in a restaurant, or owned one, young man," LuEllen scolded. "Although I guess I didn't want to visit it that badly. Something else always came up."

Cassidy reached over and squeezed her sister's hand. "I'm sorry."

LuEllen squeezed back, then released her hand. "Nothing I can do about it now."

Alex remembered something else Simon had said. "That must have been what he meant by *redemption*," she mused. They looked at her with confusion. "When I talked to Simon, he said the medallion couldn't be fake because it was his father's redemption. He said Dr. Baker had promised him it was authentic. Simon seemed quite upset by the possibility of deception."

Cassidy furrowed her eyebrows at Reid. "You told them?"

"When you raced out of the hall, Simon asked me where you were going. I told him it was to find his father because the medallion was a fake."

Cassidy sighed. "I suppose I can't blame you, considering I was about to confront Dr. Baker. I imagine this is hard on Simon. I remember hearing rumors that the Bakers were estranged for decades after the doctor was fired. It was so bad between them, Simon didn't even want to be in the same country. He ended up in India and Africa, and I heard he only recently returned to the States."

William took a drink of iced tea and coughed. "I may have had this just last night, but I'd already forgotten how potent this stuff is. You take day drinking to a whole new level, Ms. Lu."

"It's five o'clock somewhere and we've had a rough day. We're allowed."

"Not complaining, just saying. Anyway, you seem to have kept close tabs on the Bakers," William said to the couple.

"Not at first," Cassidy said, then motioned for Reid to explain.

"We started paying attention about ten years ago. Dr. Baker's name kept coming up among our colleagues, and it was always tied with Doctors Sterling and Pierce. The three became practically synonymous. That history, and the medallion itself, are why we had to be here. That, and the shrimp shack opening, of course," he said to LuEllen, almost as an afterthought.

"Of course," LuEllen dismissed. "I have no illusions about why you came. I'm just happy to see you."

"Question," Alex started, then took a much smaller sip of her drink than William had. The bourbon warmed her from within and she felt herself relax slightly. She decided to drink it slowly; she wanted to stay sharp. "What do you mean, why you *had* to be here?"

Reid gave Alex a small smile. "For one, because the doctors *weren't* mentioned in relation to this exhibit. It seemed odd."

"Downright fishy," Cassidy said. "Those two crave attention and publicity. Good, bad, doesn't matter as long as their names are in the spotlight. To not take advantage of this *alleged* discovery? Didn't make sense."

Alex could feel the tension emanating from her. The veins on Cassidy's sinewy arms grew more noticeable as she clenched her hands. This wasn't merely a professional disagreement, although

Cassidy's passion for her subject would certainly cause powerful feelings. This seemed much more personal, almost antagonistic.

Reid sat back in his chair. "For another, we knew it was impossible that someone could have found the medallion here. If they got away with that claim, it would rewrite history. Not nearly as much as what he'd intended with that blasted Diadem, but it would definitely wreak havoc."

Alex felt her phone buzz. She looked at the screen, but didn't recognize the number. "Excuse me," she said, then walked across the deck to answer the call, shielding her eyes from the sun. "Hello? This is Alex."

"Ms. Paige. How delightful. I wasn't sure I'd be able to reach you with all that unpleasantness this morning."

"I'm sorry. Who is this?" Alex had an idea who was calling, but she wanted confirmation.

"Forgive me," the silky voice replied. "This is Dr. Sterling. We met last night, and I briefly saw you again this morning."

Alex paused. William may think she noticed everything, but she certainly didn't remember everything, she scolded herself. She'd forgotten the brunette had been with Dr. Baker when they arrived at the museum. Alex took a deep breath and spoke calmly. "Yes, I remember you. How may I help you?" she leaned against the railing. William gave her a quizzical look, raising one eyebrow and tilting his head. Alex held up her index finger, silently asking him to wait.

"I think, rather, it's how I may help you," she purred. "Would you be interested in visiting the location where we found the medallion?"

"Yes," Alex said cautiously. "Of course."

"Wonderful. Since I learned you were getting a preview of the exhibit, and will also be at the opening tomorrow, I looked you up. Your passion for the past is quite pervasive. You are still going to the opening, aren't you? You and that charming friend of yours?"

Alex cleared her throat. "Possibly," she said slowly. It wasn't only Cassidy's and Reid's feelings about the woman that made her hesitant; Alex didn't trust her. Her 'spidey senses,' as William called them, were tingling.

"You simply must attend the opening, especially since you are so enthralled with history. It will be a treat to introduce you to our work. With your interest in the past, I naturally assumed you'd want to see something that changes history."

Alex remembered what Dr. Baker had said about *assuming* the night before. She didn't think it would be polite to repeat it to the woman at the other end of the line. "Is that what you're offering?" she asked. William flung his hands out, repeatedly mouthing, *Who is it?* Alex covered the phone and mouthed *Vanessa*. He rattled his head, indicating he didn't understand, so Alex tiptoed across the deck as if she was trying to navigate sand while wearing stilettos. William guffawed, then slapped his hand over his mouth.

"Ah. I hear Mr. Blake now. Yes, I am offering to show you a glimpse of something only a handful of people have seen. It would be rather cruel of me if I weren't, wouldn't it? To tease you like that? And I am definitely not a tease. Just ask Reid," she paused. "I have a feeling you're with the lovely man as we speak, considering you're friends with the elder Ms. Devereaux and the younger had quite a bit of, shall we say, excitement this morning." Her alto voice resonated seductively, despite the vaguely threatening tone of her words.

Alex shifted her gaze to Reid as she replied to the ambiguous doctor. "Where and when?"

"Decisive. I like it. I'm assuming thirty minutes will work. I'll text you the coordinates. And please, give Cassidy my regards."

The call disconnected. Alex's phone immediately buzzed. She stared at it for a few moments before returning to her seat at the table.

"What did *she* want?" Cassidy glowered.

Alex drummed her fingers, then pushed her drink across the table to William. "No more for me. I'm driving soon. Apparently, Dr. Vanessa Sterling wants to show me the dig site."

"For real?" William choked.

Reid's eyes narrowed. "Why?" he asked. The question was simple. The tone was not.

Alex shrugged. "I don't know, but I figure it's a good opportunity to ask her why she was at the museum this morning."

Cassidy grunted. "Probably to poison Harold."

LuEllen gasped. "Do you think…?"

"Don't be hasty," Reid said. "You know my feelings about both her and Gerald, but with the opening tomorrow night she had a legitimate reason to be there."

"Sure she did, to make sure they got their stories straight." Cassidy frowned. "Why would she want to meet you at the dig site? She and Gerald normally keep those tightly under wraps."

"Probably to preen, and because I'm not an expert in archaeology, I won't know what to look for." Alex pushed her chair back. "I'll find out what I can, OK?" William started to get up when Alex stopped him. "Why don't you stay here and list anyone who had a reason to hurt Harold? You know the drill."

"Means, motive, opportunity. Got it."

"I can either pick you up later, or these two could give you a ride back to Bessie," she suggested, directing the idea towards Cassidy and Reid.

LuEllen replied instead. "I think that's an excellent idea. We'll figure out who did this awful thing and make sure that Elsie Monroe doesn't cart Cass off in cuffs, and then I can drive you back, young man."

William scooted his chair back and raised his hands. "No, no, that's quite alright. I can walk. Yes, a walk sounds lovely. Or," he batted his eyelashes at Reid, "if you don't mind…"

Reid and Cassidy laughed, a delightful sound that made Alex smile, despite the circumstances. William could always ease the tension. It would be good for him to stay with the other three. Otherwise, Alex was worried Cassidy would try to take matters into her own hands. She didn't seem the type to sit still for long. Alex could relate.

She rose from the table. Cassidy followed suit, walking around Reid to grasp her hands. "Alex, please be careful. Vanessa and Gerald have no scruples. If they murdered Dr. Baker, you could be in danger."

"I'll be fine," Alex assured them all. "If she's as clever as everyone seems to think she is, she'll know that you're all aware I'm meeting her. Plus, I'm sharing my location with William. He'll be able to see where I am."

The Devereaux sisters and Reid switched their focus to William. "It's precautionary," he explained. "Alex travels solo a lot. It's safer if someone knows where she is. Especially since she's been known to have stalkers, including a totally skeevy ex-boyfriend. I'll fill you in on that after she's gone," he whispered dramatically.

Cassidy returned her gaze to Alex, gold flecks sparkling in her hazel irises. She stared intently. "Be careful. Tell her nothing. And do not trust her."

Chapter 9

A lex drove with the windows down and the moonroof open, grateful to have a few moments alone. What a terrible morning—what a terrible day it had been. The wind, carrying the salty scent of the Gulf, buffeted her hair. She knew it would turn it into a frizzy mess, but she didn't care. She took a deep breath. How was she in the middle of a murder investigation, again? She exhaled. Tapped her fingers on the steering wheel. While she had put on a brave face for William and the others, she wasn't sure meeting Vanessa was a good idea, especially since it sounded like it would just be the two of them. "I just hope Gerald's not there," Alex said out loud. That man, no matter how handsome he was, gave her the willies.

She turned down an unpaved road. Instead of the rock gravel of rural roads back home, the lane was lined with crushed shells. Trees overhung the path. The air chilled and Alex closed her windows and moonroof, muffling the cacophony of birdsong. The road twisted. Each time she neared a curve, she'd slow, concerned about meeting another vehicle. As she kept driving, she realized that probably wouldn't happen. This area was far too remote. She finally approached a clearing, empty save for a bright red Humvee. It reminded her of her ex, Ben. He'd also driven one of the monstrosities, although as a city boy he had very little need for one. Alex figured that wasn't the case with Vanessa and Gerald. Or, considering Cassidy and Reid's descriptions of the two, maybe it was.

The rumbling engine of the red giant went silent. The door opened. Vanessa exited, her long legs encased in tight-fitting cargo pants. They reminded Alex of the parachute pants she'd worn back in the '80s: plenty of pockets and very little practicality. Like the doctor's dress from the night before, it didn't look like there was room for anything besides a business card. A small one, at that.

Vanessa clipped her keys to a belt loop with a carabiner and approached Alex. "You made it. I wasn't sure you would."

"And miss a rare opportunity like this? Not on your life." Alex's enthusiasm was only slightly forced. While she didn't trust the doctor, she would rarely pass up the chance to experience a look at the distant past.

Vanessa studied her, then nodded curtly. "Interesting phrase, considering Dr. Baker's demise this morning. Come with me." She turned abruptly and led Alex towards a narrow path at the edge of the clearing. They soon emerged, and Alex shielded her eyes from the reflection of the sun off a lagoon. At its shore was a textbook dig site. At least, it looked textbook to Alex. It was the first one she'd seen in person.

"This is amazing," she said, her voice filled with awe. This time her excitement was genuine. Seeing the grids marked with stakes and string, tools organized on a table sheltered under a white canopy, and the layers of exposed earth transported Alex to another world. She knew it transported the archaeologists to another time.

"It is, isn't it? I always forget how it must seem to someone new. It's so easy to become inured when this," Vanessa said, sweeping her arm across the site, "is your job."

Her tone, laced with barely disguised disgust, surprised Alex. "This is where you found the medallion?"

"Straight to the point. Like I said earlier, you're direct. I like that. At least, I respect it. So many people try to hedge; they never say what they really mean." Vanessa walked on a narrow path between excavated pits. She didn't tell Alex to follow her, assuming she would. "Here," she pointed to one of the deeper cavities. "This is where we found it. You can see the strata. Would you like a closer look? Good. Be careful."

Alex followed her advice, mindfully lifting her legs, one after the other, over the string marking a section of the grid and then descending a wooden ladder. The hole was deep. When she reached the bottom, she could barely see out. She squatted, resting her hand against the wall and raking her eyes over its rough surface. A spot of blue caught her eyes. "Is that what I think it is?" she exclaimed, pointing to what looked like a bead.

Vanessa languidly peered at the spot Alex indicated, then turned to her with a smug look on her face. "That, my dear, is exactly what you think it is." She began brushing the surrounding earth away with her talon-like fingernails, gradually easing the artifact from the earth. She finally pulled it out and placed it in Alex's palm.

The artifact sat in the center of her hand. It was slightly tapered and shaped like a tiny, ornamental barrel. Alex lifted her hand so she could get a closer look. The glass bead was hollow. Its central color was a rich blue. The ends were decorated with layers of white and red stripes, forming a ring of inverted Vs. Vanessa took the artifact from her palm and Alex realized she'd been holding her breath.

"That," Vanessa said, holding the artifact up to the sun, "is a chevron bead. These first appeared in the 15th century in Venice and Murano. Its presence, along with several implements we've also found, is how we know de Soto's expedition made it here. They're indicative of the inventory he and the explorers took with them. The savages they encountered loved these little trinkets."

Alex bristled. Although she'd planned to avoid engaging Vanessa beyond gathering information, she couldn't help herself from responding. "My understanding is that the tribes the first Europeans encountered were much more advanced civilizations than De Soto and others assumed."

"Lies!" Vanessa hissed. "You call a dirt mound civilization? Thatched huts, civilization? Primitives. They were all primitives. Columbus. De Soto. De León. Coronado… They brought order. They brought discipline. They brought beauty," she said, brandishing the colorful bead, holding it within an inch of Alex's eyes.

Alex resisted rearing back. She knew if she flinched in any way, this woman whose chest heaved with the exertion of her passion would see it as weakness. "It is beautiful," she said, as diplomatically as she could.

"Yes, yes it is. And we've found dozens of them on this site."

"Where was the medallion?"

"I discovered *El Beso de la Muerta* right there," Vanessa said, pointing to a rectangular alcove. A numbered marker sat inside, and Alex figured that's how they cataloged the artifacts. "See how it's at the same stratum as the bead? That's how we could determine its age."

"I'm surprised you missed finding the bead during your excavating," Alex said.

"Who says I did?"

"Oh, I get it. Like one of those gem mining tourist attractions."

Vanessa advanced on Alex until she had no option but to back up or be knocked over. "Are you questioning my integrity?" Vanessa seethed.

Alex may have had to step back, but she refused to be bullied. She glared at the brunette. "Should I be?"

Vanessa threw her hand back, still holding the bead, as if to strike. "Dr. Vanessa Sterling," a man's voice boomed. "What have I told you about hitting journalists?" She slowly lowered her hand and Gerald appeared on the wall above and behind Vanessa. "Please forgive my wife," he said. "As I mentioned last night, she gets rather put out prior to a big exhibit."

Alex glared, focusing on the woman with her in the pit, then switched to the man looking down on them. Although Vanessa had complimented her for being direct, Alex didn't think now was the time to tell them what she really thought, but she couldn't help challenging them a little. "I found a bead as soon as I got down here," she explained to Gerald. "Dr. Sterling was just about to tell me why it was left intact instead of being excavated like the rest." Alex suddenly had the urge to check her phone and see if she had service. It wouldn't be good to be stuck without GPS with no way for William to see where she was. She knew, however, removing her eyes from Dr. Price's would be a mistake.

Scorn emanated from him. He inhaled, held his breath, then exhaled, like a professor dealing with a willfully ignorant student. Then he laughed, a sound without mirth. "Dear Ms. Paige. I remember you saying something about not knowing much about archaeology? Well, then I suggest you leave it to the professionals. Dr. Sterling did you a great favor by bringing you out here. It would be incredibly disappointing if she regretted it because you've been disrespectful."

Alex held his gaze. "No disrespect intended. Curiosity is a hazard of my profession."

"Try not to make it unnecessarily hazardous."

"As someone who knows so little," Alex said, trying to placate the two of them, "I would appreciate it if you'd educate me."

Vanessa relaxed. "That wasn't so hard, was it?" The switch was so immediate, and so complete, Alex shuddered. Ignoring her reaction, Vanessa explained the rigorous methodology archaeologists used to excavate and record sites. As she talked, she climbed the ladder out of the pit. Alex followed her, murmuring in the appropriate places.

"Fascinating," Alex finally said. "It's no wonder you and your findings are so well known." She finally looked at her phone, relieved to see she had a strong signal. "I'm sorry, but I didn't realize what time it was. I have another appointment. Thank you for your time and for giving me this exclusive look at your work," she said, sweeping her arms around the dig site.

Gerald casually blocked her way to the narrow path that led to the parking lot. She stood in front of him, maintaining eye contact. He lifted one corner of his mouth. "I hope it was educational," he said, then turned around and walked the narrow trail to their vehicles. She heard Vanessa behind her and Alex walked between the doctors, her spidey senses screaming like a Midwestern tornado warning. As soon as they reached the clearing, Alex made a beeline for her Subaru, unlocking it as she neared and only turning to the two doctors once she opened her door and stood behind it. "Thank you again for this opportunity. I realize you don't invite many people to see your sites, especially lay people like me." The doctors, standing side by side with their hands on their hips, nodded simultaneously. "Well then. I'll see you tomorrow!" Alex said with false bravado before closing her door, starting the engine, and backing away.

Her bravado disappeared as soon as she put her foot on the accelerator. Alex raced out of the lot, kicking up sand and crushed shells. She took a turn too fast; her Outback slid around one of the sharp curves, nearly skidding off the narrow road. Alex took her foot off the gas and her car came to a stop. She breathed deeply and willed her heart rate to calm down. After resting a few moments, she resumed driving, this time at a much more reasonable speed. Her phone rang.

"I see you're on the move again," William said. Alex let out the breath she didn't realize she'd been holding. She seemed to do that a lot around the two doctors. "Did you enjoy your visit with the temperamental Dr. Vanessa Sterling?"

"Temperamental is one way to put it. I thought she was going to stab me with those knives for nails she's got."

William sucked in air. "Are you OK? What happened? Do I need to come get you?"

"I'm fine, really. But according to Dr. Sterling and her husband, I impugned her integrity. In my defense, she called Native Americans 'savages.'"

William gasped. "She said *what?* I'm surprised you didn't punch her."

Alex reached the end of the gravel road and stopped. "It was hard not to. Where are you?"

"I'm at the Shack with Cassidy and Reid right now. We'll pick up some grub and meet you at your condo."

"Perfect," Alex said, realizing how hungry she was; she hadn't eaten since breakfast this morning before leaving for the museum. *Was that only this morning?* she thought. It seemed like ages ago. "I have a lot to tell you."

"I'm sure you do. Wait a minute," William commanded. "What do you mean, her *and* her husband? Gerald was there?"

Alex could hear the concern in his voice. "Yes, and he's even more volatile than she is. Every phrase is a minefield."

"Booby-trapped like an ancient temple, eh?"

"Pretty much. I'm nearly back to the condo. Come on up when you guys get there."

"Deal."

Alex hung up and thought about her experience with the two doctors. She consciously eased the tension from her shoulders and loosened her grip on the steering wheel. If they knew the chevron bead was there, and there's no way they could have missed it, why would they leave it? Could they have been so focused on the medallion they didn't think it was worth digging out? Or maybe they left it for people like Alex, as an illustration of the timeline, and to give the feeling of discovery. The latter was the more logical explanation, but after spending even a short amount of time with Dr. Sterling and Dr. Price, Alex wasn't positive much about them was logical. They seemed to run on turmoil and drama.

Chapter 10

Alex smelled creole spices and heard muffled conversation. She opened the door to her condo to see Reid with his hand raised as if to knock. Cassidy and William peered around either shoulder. All three carried bags of food. "Bring that in here," she said. "I started drooling the moment you got off the elevator."

They opened the containers and began serving up a variety of entrees and sides on the plates Alex had set on the breakfast bar. After they'd loaded up, they headed to the balcony. Cassidy curled up cross-legged on the outdoor couch. Reid sat next to her, and William took one of the large swivel chairs to the side. He offered to split his sandwich, pulling a pocketknife out of his cargo shorts and cutting it in half.

"There are knives in the kitchen," Alex said.

"Yes, I know, but I didn't have to get up to use this. Now say thank you."

"Thank you," she said, then scooted over a chaise lounge and arranged her plate on the cushion in front of her. They all began talking at once, then laughed. "You go first, Alex," Cassidy said, then stabbed a scallop with a fork and popped it in her mouth. "William told us some. Sounds like you got a prime taste of the doctors."

"You could say that again. Those two change moods faster than Chicago weather."

Reid nodded. "Vanessa's always been rather hotheaded."

"Always?" William asked around a cajun french fry. He coughed at the spice and grabbed for the ice water Alex had set on the table before they arrived.

Cassidy sighed. "I suppose you'll find out anyway, so we might as well tell you."

"Not that it's a secret," Reid said.

"No, but it's not something we want to advertise. Anyway, in his college days, Reid here had the hots for none other than Ms. Vanessa Sterling. Before she became a so-called 'doctor.'"

"You and V, sittin' in a tree? Do tell," William said, leaning forward and pointing a new french fry at Reid.

Reid shook his head. "Not much to tell. We dated. We broke up."

"And *why* did you break up?" Cassidy prompted.

The movie star look-alike closed his eyes, an expression of long-suffering on his face. When he opened them, though, he looked at his partner and smiled. "Because she's an icky lying scammer face."

William giggled with glee. "You sound just like me!"

"What happened?" Alex asked.

"She wanted me to help her fudge some research for her dissertation. When I refused, she said it wasn't harming anyone. *Except for those of us who do real research*, I replied." He rubbed his cheek. "She slapped me. I walked out. I'm no boy scout, but I couldn't stomach someone with that level of moral ambiguity."

"You kinda seem like a boy scout to me," William said with a wink.

"Most of the time, he is," Cassidy agreed, "but Vanessa can get anyone riled up. Besides, in addition to hurting people who put in the work, she's more than willing to destroy the narratives of people who can't tell their own stories. Plus, she hit you," Cassidy said, reaching over to take Reid's hand.

"That, too."

"Alex, why don't you fill us in and then we'll tell you what we discussed. I have a suspicion our impressions might line up," Cassidy said.

"Sure. But before I do, have you heard any more from Detective Monroe?"

"No. I don't expect to until tomorrow. Lu told me Elsie's got a standing Friday night dinner date with her daughter, and there'd have to be a Cat-5 for her to miss it. Now, tell us everything you can remember about this dig site and what Vanessa and Gerald said to you."

Alex closed her eyes, recalling the layout of the site. She described it in detail, especially the pit where Vanessa claimed they'd found the medallion. "She called it *El Beso de la Muerte*. The kiss of death?"

"What is it with all these *de la muertes*?" William asked. "The tree of death, the kiss of death. One would think we've walked into a big horror movie."

"People at that time probably thought they had," Cassidy said. She met Reid's eyes. "Are you thinking what I'm thinking?" He nodded while dunking grilled prawn into a red pepper aioli. He took a bite and Cassidy explained while he chewed. "It sounds like they seeded the site."

"You mean they planted those beads to make it look like a real dig?" Alex asked.

Cassidy cocked her finger like a gun. "Exactly."

Alex leaned back in the lounge chair and watched a seagull float past. Occasionally she'd hear children's laughter from the beach far below. *I will take a vacation*, she promised herself, *just as soon as we figure this out.* "I hinted at that, actually. Likened it to a gem mining tourist attraction."

Cassidy gasped. "You did not."

"I did, and almost got slapped myself." Alex paused. "Do you think Dr. Baker knew?"

"That's the burning question," Reid answered. "We did our homework, like you asked. William, do you have our notes about our potential suspects?"

William took a bite of his po' boy while bending over to unzip his backpack and pulling out a spiral-bound notebook. After flipping to a page marked in columns, he handed it to Alex.

The list of potential suspects was short. Vanessa Sterling, Gerald Price, Cassidy Devereaux, Reid McKinley, Simon Baker, and Alex Paige. Alex's head snapped up. "Me?"

William smiled sheepishly. "You knew what a manchineel was."

"Good point," she conceded. "What about Simon? You've got a question mark for motive."

"Yes, but he definitely had the means and the opportunity, more so than anyone else," Reid said.

"Except Vanessa. Remember, she was with Dr. Baker this morning. I bet she slipped something into his drink before she left."

Cassidy's certainty was convincing, Alex thought, and after this afternoon she wouldn't put murder past Vanessa, but if they were going to convince Detectives Monroe and Washington, they would need something besides convenient timing and dislike.

"There's no motive for Vanessa and Gerald, either," Alex pointed out.

"I know," Cassidy slumped. "These two shot down every idea I had. Said they were too *far-fetched*."

Alex grabbed her empty plate and got up to take it to the kitchen. "I might have something that can help," she said, accepting Reid's plate as well.

William scarfed the last of his sandwich and stacked Cassidy's plate on his. He trailed Alex towards the kitchen. "Would you be referring to that picture I saw you sneak earlier in Dr. Baker's office?"

"I would," Alex said. She rinsed the plates, put them in the dishwasher, and dried her hands. She motioned for William to go back out to the balcony and she followed, pulling her phone out of her back pocket.

"So what was it?" he asked, prompting Cassidy and Reid to look up. "What'd you find?"

"Names," Alex said. She pulled up the photo she'd taken of the paper after she'd returned the stack that had fallen from his desk that morning. "While I was waiting for you, I looked up a few of these. They all seem to have one thing in common."

Cassidy took the phone from Alex. Her eyes narrowed, and she handed it to Reid. "Exactly as we thought."

"Care to fill me in?" William asked.

Reid passed the phone to William. The image displayed a list of names and numbers. Some of them had been marked through, and some had checkboxes drawn in the margin. "These are antiquities dealers," Reid explained. "Some legitimate. Some not."

"Most of them are not," Cassidy said.

Alex nodded. "That's what I found. I recognized one from a story I'd done, and several of the others have been charged with dealing in stolen artifacts or with trying to sell fake ones. Those fauxtiquities, as you called them."

"Why would Dr. Baker have a list of people like that?" William asked, then raised his hands when the other three looked at him with surprise. "Duh. I guess it's obvious. He planned to sell the medallion, right?"

"It sure seems like it," Cassidy said.

"If he had, he would have gotten quite the shock." Reid frowned. "The real medallion does have an alleged curse attached to it, but it certainly never made it to Alabama. And it isn't even Spanish."

"How can you be so certain?" Alex asked.

"Well," Reid drew out the word. "We happen to know where it was found, and that it was stolen several years ago."

William's face eloquently expressed his doubt. "Why would they try to pawn off something like that? They had to know you'd know it was stolen, and that they didn't find it here."

"Maybe, maybe not," Alex said. "You'd be surprised how many stolen antiquities end up in museums and for sale with legitimate auction houses."

Cassidy nodded. "It's a multi-billion dollar business. But how did you know?"

"That story I mentioned. During my newspaper days, I investigated a supposed philanthropist and collector. He bought hundreds, perhaps thousands, of stolen relics. Got off with a slap on the wrist."

Reid snapped his fingers. "Stanhope," he said. "He worked out a deal where his only punishment was to never buy antiquities again."

Cassidy's expression had darkened during the exchange. "For someone like him, who thinks he can own whatever he wants, that *is* punishment. I guarantee he's still at it."

"Do you think he's involved in this?" William asked.

They shrugged. Reid answered. "Maybe. If the story about the medallion was true, it's definitely a piece Stanhope would want to add to his collection."

Alex picked up the notebook containing their suspects' names. She grabbed the pen and wrote *Stanhope*, then added *Greed* under the column for Motive. "You said you knew it was stolen. How, and how could they have not known you'd know as soon as you saw it?"

Cassidy and Reid exchanged one of their secret looks. Alex interpreted it. "I'm guessing they *didn't* think you'd know about it. They also didn't think you'd be here. That's why they were so mad you were at LuEllen's opening, and even more mad about Dr. Baker offering to give you a preview."

"You're mostly correct," Cassidy said. "They certainly didn't think we'd be here. We have been in Guatemala—Vanessa was right about that."

"And they didn't think we'd have any way of knowing the real medallion had been stolen, or where it was originally found," Reid continued.

William frowned. "Now correct me if I'm wrong, but from what I've gathered, yours is a pretty small community. I have a feeling gossip flies faster than a Concord."

"That's true, but in this instance, everything surrounding the medallion was kept tightly under wraps."

"Ah. To talk about it would have been *el beso de la muerte*," William quipped.

Cassidy shook her head. "First of all, that's not the artifact's name, nor has it ever been."

"But William's not really wrong. Let's just say the person from whom it was stolen didn't exactly want its disappearance publicized," Reid explained.

Alex sat back in the chaise lounge and crossed her arms. "Ahhh, got it. The theft was never disclosed."

"Correct."

"So how did you two know about it?" William asked.

"Because we're the ones who found it."

Alex stared at Reid, dumbfounded by this development. "That's fairly important information to know. How did it end up in someone's private collection?"

"It was our client," Cassidy answered. "He hired us to dig on his property. We made this incredible discovery, the medallion. We tried to get him to give it to a museum, make it available to the public, but he refused. Then it was stolen and this client had the audacity to ask us to find it."

"Did you? Find it?"

Reid shook his head. "No. We searched for months. You might even say we're still searching."

"What's in Dr. Baker's museum, then, if it's not the relic you found?"

"Before the medallion was stolen, the client had a copy made. Two, actually. He gave one to us. In case we ever found the real McCoy, we could replace it with a fake and whoever had it would never be the wiser. Apparently, he made replicas of all his ill-begotten goods. There were so many, he kept a forger on retainer."

"So that's why you were checking it out so closely. To see if it was one of the duplicates," Alex stated. It wasn't a question.

Cassidy nodded, then got up and crossed the balcony to the railing before turning around to face them. "There are minute etchings on the back of the real medallion. You can't see them without magnification. The version in Dr. Baker's museum doesn't have them."

William grew pensive. "What if…Harold discovers, somehow, he's got another fauxtiquity on his hands. He confronts Vanessa, tries to blackmail her, she denies it and sees the other *de la muerte* in the courtyard. Offers to make tea for the dear doctor and slips a little poison into his cup. Boom. Crime of opportunity."

The archaeologists exchanged a glance. Reid answered. "Maybe. This isn't the first time Vanessa and Gerald have faked a find. But they always manufactured locations, not the actual antiquities. Either way, we have no proof."

"I'd say we do," Cassidy interrupted. "Vanessa was with him right before he died. She could have made tea, or slipped something in his coffee or whatever he was drinking, right before leaving. You saw how easy it was to get to that courtyard. Apples are falling off those branches like Newton had a permanent chair under it."

Alex shivered at the imagery, thinking of what the poisonous tree could do to a person. Reid focused on Cassidy. He waited a few beats before replying. "It's suggestive, I'll give you that, but we don't have *definitive* proof. Why don't we take a look at that list of names Alex found? If Harold was planning to sell the medallion, that's a good place to start."

Alex got up and paced back and forth. Cassidy opened her mouth to speak, but William subtly shushed her with an index finger to his lips. He knew when Alex was working up to an insight.

She stopped. "Maybe–now hear me out–maybe Dr. Baker wasn't planning to blackmail them."

William caught on. "Maybe he planned to expose the doctors."

"Because Simon was home, and this was his redemption."

"And Harold confronted them."

"And *now* we have our motive." Alex and William grinned at each other.

Chapter 11

Cassidy tilted her head slightly. "You're thinking Dr. Baker had those names because he thought their story was a bunch of hooey? Reid? What do you think?"

He nodded slowly. "It could work. Although he and Vanessa were pretty chummy when we got to the museum this morning."

"Were they?" Alex asked. "I thought I detected some tension. Of course, that could just be hindsight and wishful thinking." She sat back down on the lounge, but she didn't recline. Instead, she leaned forward with her elbows on her knees. She rapidly tapped her heel. "Let me get this straight. Vanessa and Gerald presented Dr. Baker with a medallion they supposedly found near Oyster Bay. They convinced him it proved de Soto's expedition came here."

"With his fascination with the conquistadors, he'd be an easy target," Cassidy spat.

"So he bought their story, but as the opening of the exhibition neared, what, he got nervous?"

William inhaled sharply and snapped his fingers in Cassidy's direction. "I bet LuEllen told him she wished you were coming and he remembered you were the one who'd found him out, oh so long ago," he said to Cassidy.

She mulled over the idea. "Maybe. Which might have prompted him to actually get verification this time."

"Something doesn't line up." Alex looked directly at Cassidy. "If you found the medallion in the first place, why in the world would Vanessa and Gerald risk showing it publicly? Wouldn't they know its provenance? I can't imagine you would have kept quiet about a discovery like that."

Cassidy closed her eyes and inhaled deeply. A slight pink infused her tan cheeks, and Alex realized the other woman was blushing. Cassidy exhaled, then turned to Reid. He squeezed his partner's hand. "This is embarrassing," he said. "Not only did our client not want anyone to know about its theft, he didn't want anyone to know about it at all. We literally couldn't tell anyone about the find, or about the entire dig." He noticed the confused looks on Alex's and William's faces. "It was our first private job."

"We'd always worked with universities," Cassidy explained.

"An anonymous client contacted us and presented an unbelievable offer. Which we shouldn't have believed, but we did."

"I'd been wanting to excavate that site for years," Cassidy said wistfully, "but it's on private land. And then the money, wow, the money was too much to resist."

"Who was it?" Alex asked her.

"We don't know. We never met, and all conversations were via an anonymous email. Anyway, we signed what we thought was a standard contract."

"Like gullible fools, we didn't have an attorney review it," Reid said bitterly. This time, Cassidy squeezed his hand. "There was a cleverly worded codicil dictating our silence. We couldn't tell a soul."

"Nobody knew we'd found the medallion, or anything else from that site. Nobody, except the client and whomever they shared it with, even knew it existed." Cassidy stood and paced. "I bet if we check, we'll find out there was a black market auction a few months before they contacted Dr. Baker."

"Do you think they know it's a fake? You know them," William said. "Would they be the type to brazenly put something fake on display, at a very public museum exhibition, no less? On second thought, I've met them, and I'm betting they're perfectly capable of that level of duplicity."

Cassidy shook her head. "I wouldn't put much past those two, but Vanessa really is a genius, and Gerald's no slouch. They wouldn't be stupid enough to seed a replica at a site. They probably got the medallion from one of those dealers," she said, tapping the screen of Alex's phone, "and thought it was authentic. Stolen, but authentic."

As they talked, the sun dropped lower on the horizon. They were soon awash in the reds of sunset. Reid looked at his watch, then spoke to Alex. "Could you send me that list? We can put some feelers out, see if any of the legitimate dealers know anything about it."

"Of course. But be careful. After covering the Stanhope debacle, I learned people like that will do anything to protect themselves. If they think you'll cause them trouble, they'll retaliate."

Cassidy stood up, smiling sadly. "Oh, believe me, we know. There's a reason we now vet our private clients quite vigorously."

"Speaking of which," William said, following the couple into the condo, "what happened with your client? Should we be concerned they'll hear about the exhibit and show up, guns blazing, so to speak?"

Reid and Cassidy paused at the door, turning as one to face William and Alex. "Yes," Reid said. "We should be very concerned."

Alex sat on the outdoor couch and stretched her legs on the coffee table. On the way back to the balcony, she'd grabbed a couple of stemless glasses and a bottle of pinot noir. William gracefully flopped down next to her. He was the only person she knew who could flop gracefully, although Cassidy and Reid came close. Alex poured each of them a glass. They focused on the horizon, both lost in their thoughts. The sky subtly shifted colors as the sun dipped closer to the edge of the earth. "What are you thinking?" he asked. "Your disco ball for a brain is blinding me."

"It's definitely a party up here," she said, tapping her temple. "This has become much more complicated."

"Tell me about it. I thought we had a simple case of greed and murder."

"Murder is rarely simple."

"True." William agreed. "Let's recap, if you wouldn't mind. It's been a long day and my brain feels like a Pachinko machine."

Alex took a sip of her wine, then set the plastic tumbler on the coffee table. "Let me see if I've got this right. Many years ago, we don't know how long, a mystery man hired Cassidy and Reid to dig for buried treasure on his land. They signed a contract, but it was probably with a dummy corporation and they were young and naive. So, they sign it, search, and voila, they find treasure in the shape of a gold and pearl medallion."

"They never mentioned where this was, did they?"

"Nope. I'll have to ask." She picked up a pen and jotted a reminder in the notebook. "Sometime after they found this, and realized they couldn't tell a soul, which I'm thinking must have been pure torture, the medallion went missing. Mystery man hires them to find it again, but no luck."

"Fast forward," William picked up the thread. "There's a private auction open only to unsavory types like Drs. Sterling and Price. They place the winning bid on this gorgeous medallion. The provided provenance, which claims it was part of de Soto's expedition, seems legit, because despite their proclivity towards unethical shortcuts, they're too smart to pawn off something that could be proven as fake."

"I'm betting that's a case of Gestalt. They wanted it to be real, therefore it was," Alex considered. "This is all supposition, of course, but it makes sense." They continued the timeline: Vanessa and Gerald approached Dr. Baker, knowing of his obsession with the early Spaniards and their exploration of the Americas. They also knew about his unusual passion for cursed items.

"I can picture it," William said. "He would have been darn near giddy to get his hands on something like that. If he found out it was a fake..."

"It could have destroyed him. From what Simon said, and from LuEllen's reaction to him, it seems like he really was turning over a new leaf, as they say."

"He confronts Ms. Femme Fatale, which turns fatal."

"Nice wordplay," Alex smiled. "Now all we have to do is convince Detective Monroe."

"Maybe her partner would be easier. He's certainly easier on the eyes." He wiggled his eyebrows.

"We'll sleep on it and touch base in the morning. I know, I know, not too early."

William laced his fingers and rested them on his flat stomach. "You're seeing the canal tomorrow?"

"That's the plan."

"I'm sorry."

Alex raised her head and looked at her friend. "For what?"

William took her hand. "I know you were excited about seeing LuEllen, about seeing this canal, and maybe even relaxing. You were looking for things to get back to normal, and now it's overshadowed."

She shrugged. "I'm beginning to realize there is no normal. Besides," she brightened, "the amateur archaeologist who discovered the canal is giving me the tour. I can ask him about Vanessa and Gerald's dig site."

"I noticed we've stopped calling them by their honorific."

"It affords a level of respect I'm not willing to give them," Alex said.

"Do you think she killed him?"

Alex gazed at the sea, its waves shimmering in the last rays of the setting sun. "She's the most obvious choice. But, I've been wrong before." She bent over to pick up the notebook, reading through the list of suspects again. At the bottom, she added *Mystery Client*, and under Motivation, she wrote *Revenge*.

Alex's alarm didn't have a chance to ring before the smell of Bushwacker coffee awakened her. She'd set the coffee maker prior to going to bed to make sure her morning would start seamlessly. It was still dark when she opened the sliding glass door to the balcony. She rested her arms on the railing for a few minutes, inhaling the briny air and treasuring the slight breeze ruffling her hair. She relished this feeling of tranquility, of peace, knowing it would need to carry her through the day. What would it bring? Would she learn something from Jacob Rex, the amateur archaeologist she was meeting that morning, that would definitively point to Vanessa and Gerald? She swallowed a sip of coffee and told herself to focus on the wonder of seeing the canal itself. She couldn't get so wrapped up in Dr. Baker's murder that she forgot everything else.

She moved to the couch, placing her coffee mug on the end table. She set her timer. If she didn't give herself a time limit, she'd be hunched over with pen in hand for hours. Alex picked up her journal and started writing. Her morning ritual—coffee, deep breaths, and her journal—kept her sane. It's how she processed the world, how she made sense of the disparate thoughts that danced in her brain like, as William often said, a disco ball. It was never a simple listing of ideas. There was no line from A to B to Z. Instead, it was like a pointillism painting. Up close, it looked like a bunch of random dots. Step back, and a picture emerged.

Her timer buzzed. She put her pen down. It was going to be a busy day, one most likely visited by confrontation and potential danger. But now she was ready to meet it head on.

Chapter 12

Alex quickly got ready, putting on cargo pants and a long-sleeved t-shirt. Fortunately, while it was supposed to be sunny that day, it would be in the low sixties. Perfect weather to go see an ancient canal in the woods. She double-checked her bag: bug spray, sunscreen, and all her reporting essentials. Before walking out the front door, Alex walked to the balcony for one more gaze at the Gulf. While her Lincoln Park condo back home looked out over a harbor and Lake Michigan, there was something about knowing this was the end of the United States. Beyond the vast expanse of sea were island countries. It gave her a feeling of perspective.

It was still early. The sun had crested the horizon, but hadn't gotten far. A gull flew by at eye level. "It's just you and me this morning," she said with a smile. Movement from far below caught her eye. "Or maybe not." Alex realized it was Zoe, the young woman who created sand castles for a living. Something clicked. Alex ran into the condo, sliding on her socks before turning back to close the glass doors. She grabbed her bag, slipped into her shoes, and raced out.

The elevator reached the first floor. The doors barely opened before Alex squeezed through them. She darted across the lobby, pushed open the doors that led to the pool and the beach, making a hard right to get to the boardwalk path. By the time she reached the sand, she needed to stop for a moment to collect herself. She didn't want to approach the young woman in her harried state. She swept the beach and breathed a sigh of relief. Zoe was still there. Alex calmed down, then walked towards her.

"Good morning," Zoe called without looking up from her sculpture. "You're an early riser, too?"

"Always, to my friend William's chagrin. He thinks there's something distinctly wrong with me."

Zoe put down the plastic scraper she'd been using to shape what looked like a tail. "Let him think that. Fewer people who know this magic, the fewer we have to share it with."

"What are you creating?" Alex asked. "Looks like it might be an alligator."

"Ding ding ding. LuEllen loved the shrimp so much, she commissioned me to do this one."

"Ah, for her Gator Gumbo Bites, right?"

"Exactly." Zoe stood up and dusted sand from her board shorts. She squinted into the rising sun. "For some reason, I don't think you rushed down here to ask me about my work." She turned to Alex. "I heard you thumping on the boardwalk. You seemed to be in a bit of a hurry."

"You would be correct," Alex said. "I have what may seem like an odd question."

"Shoot."

"Is Elsie Monroe your mother?" Alex held her breath while she waited. It had come to her in a flash as soon as she saw the sculptor on the beach. She'd pictured the card the young woman had given her: Zoe Monroe, Sand Artist.

Zoe's shoulders lowered slightly, not enough to be a slump, but enough for Alex to notice. "Why do you ask?"

Alex felt the tension emanating from her. She decided to be open. "You heard about Dr. Baker?" When Zoe nodded, Alex continued. "Your mother is leading the investigation, and she's convinced Cassidy," she gestured to the alligator's tail, "LuEllen's sister, is the murderer. She won't even consider anyone else."

Zoe raised her chin, closed her eyes, and scrunched her lips together before speaking. She opened her eyes and looked off at the horizon. "That's because Detective Monroe cannot stand her. If I had a dime for every time I heard her complain about 'those Devereauxs,' I'd own one of those condos," she said, pointing up at the high-rise behind them.

"She seems to be OK with LuEllen."

"Ha! That's because LuEllen looks like a sweet old lady, and she didn't 'ruin her life.'" Zoe used air quotes.

Now they were getting to it, Alex thought. "How did Cassidy ruin your mother's life?"

"She stole her dream. Heard that over, and over, and over growing up. There's a reason I moved out as soon as I hit eighteen. Couldn't handle it anymore. She just couldn't let it go. I've tried to tell her, hey Mom, you're a detective. That's pretty darn impressive, and you did that yourself. Let some stupid talent show go. You were six years old, for freaking sake." Zoe stopped, then narrowed her eyes at Alex. "What kind of voodoo are you? I have never told anyone this."

Alex smiled and shrugged. "It's a gift. People talk to me."

"I guess so. I hope you use your powers for good."

"Most of the time," she winked. "So this all stems back to a talent show?"

"Can you believe it? It's been decades, and Mom *still* hates Cassidy. Totally ridiculous. And totally mean."

"So what happened?" Alex prompted. She refrained from looking at her watch. She didn't want to be late for her appointment at the canal, but she figured she had some time before she had to leave.

"You heard Mr. and Mrs. Devereaux were killed in a car accident?" When Alex nodded, Zoe continued. "Can you imagine? Cassidy was only five. Growing up it was only mom and me, and we don't exactly get along, but I can't imagine being an orphan. At least she had LuEllen. Anyway, there was this big county-wide talent show. From what Mom's told me, over and over and over, she was a shoo-in. She'd been taking tap dance lessons for three years, and *Mrs. Jones said I was a natural*," Zoe mimicked. "Grandma didn't seem like a stage mom to me, but I guess she was. So the county has this big show. Mom's all ready. Got her outfit. She'd been collecting glass bottles and returning them for the deposit for months so she could pay for it. Had her routine down. Then Cassidy's parents up and die, she's an orphan, she reads a 'stupid poem'," –more air quotes– "and they give the trophy to *poor little miss sunshine*."

Zoe shuddered and took a breath. "I still hear that story every Christmas. And since LuEllen's hired me for stuff like this, Mom decides to show up occasionally just to ask if I've heard anything about Cassidy. Best thing she could have done was get out of here, and away from Mom, when she had the chance."

Alex thought about what Zoe had told her. She chewed her lower lip. "That's a long time to hold on to a grudge."

Zoe shrugged. "I guess Mom had it pretty rough growing up. I never knew my grandpa. In and out of trouble. Ended up dying in prison before I was born."

Alex refused to give the young woman a look of sympathy. She knew it would be interpreted as pity. That's not what Alex felt, nor what Zoe wanted.

"That talent show was mom's way out, she said. There were scouts from Disney there. She was going to be the next Shirley Temple, or whoever was big back in the '80s." Zoe said it like it was centuries ago, not just a few decades. "After that, she made it her mission to prove she was better than Cassidy. Ten years later, I came along. She even blamed her for that, as if she's the one who got her pregnant." Zoe gave her a sidelong look again. "Voodoo. I swear. You put a spell on me or something, didn't you?"

Alex chuckled. "Nope. It's my super power. But I do promise you, I do only use it for good."

"You're not going to get my mom in trouble, are you? She is a good detective, I swear." At that moment, Zoe seemed shy and uncertain, a daughter afraid for her mother and not the independent entrepreneur who'd left home as a teenager.

"I don't plan to," she said, then amended it when Zoe looked at her with concern. "No, I won't get her in trouble. Now that I understand her better, I may be able to convince her to look at other suspects."

"You don't think Cassidy did it? Mom said she was pretty upset with Dr. Baker about this exhibit, said she couldn't see straight when it came to anything with the Spanish. She had it all worked out."

Alex shook her head. "I was there. Cassidy didn't have time."

"What about before you got there? She could have done it then, couldn't she?"

"Dr. Sterling was at the museum when we arrived, and those two can't be in the same place or the building will implode." Alex surprised herself by how much she was telling her. *Seems like Zoe's got a little of her own voodoo*, she thought.

"Oooh, I've seen her. She looks like Jessica Rabbit if she were a werewolf. Not someone I'd want to tangle with."

"Nor would I. Hey, Zoe? Thank you. I can tell you love your mom and you're proud of her."

Zoe looked down at the sand at her feet and sighed. "I just wish she could see what I see."

Alex reached over and squeezed the young woman's shoulder. "I promise not to get her in trouble, OK?" When Zoe nodded, Alex turned and walked back towards the boardwalk.

Chapter 13

"Well, hello there, pretty lady! You must be Alex Paige." A man wearing a long-sleeved plaid shirt and neatly creased jeans climbed down from a rusted tan Chevy pickup. He walked towards Alex across the small parking area that was more weeds than gravel with his hand held out.

She shook it. His leathery skin spoke of a man who worked outside. "And you, sir, must be Jacob Rex."

"One and the same, one and the same. So," he said, sticking his thumbs in his front pockets, "you're curious about our little old canal here, eh? And I do mean old," he chuckled.

"You could say that again."

"You're curious about our... just joshin' you. C'mon then. Follow me." He reached into the cab of his truck and put a ball cap on his thin white hair.

Alex read the lettering on the front of his hat indicating Jacob was a Vietnam vet. "Thank you for your service, Sir."

"My pleasure, ma'am. Although I can tell you, serving was no pleasure of mine. Didn't want to be there in the first place, but I was, and I came back, thank the good Lord. But that's ancient history. Not as ancient as this here canal, though, eh?" Jacob chuckled again and Alex couldn't help but laugh with him. She was instantly drawn to his warmth and openness.

Jacob led her across the gravel towards a wall of tall grasses. She couldn't see a break in the growth, but he knew exactly where he was going, and she followed him to a narrow path.

He walked nimbly through the tangle of thick overgrowth. "You mentioned in your email you're here because of LuEllen?"

"Yes, sir," Alex said, watching her feet to make sure she didn't stumble on any tree roots. "I wanted to help celebrate her opening and figured while I'm here I should explore. When I came across news of the canal, I knew I had to see it."

"Well, young lady, you're in for a treat. I've gotta ask—did you try one of Lu's Gator Gumbo Bites?"

Alex coughed. "I certainly did."

Jacob laughed. "And you survived to tell the tale. That LuEllen's a good one. Been through a lot, especially with her sister. Met her?" He turned to look at Alex while holding back a branch that stretched across the path. She nodded. "Happy to see that wild thing's calmed down some. Although, can't say she's actually calmed any. More like she's found her direction. Whelp, here we are." They stopped at the edge of a clearing, Jacob with his hands on his hips and a giant grin on his face.

Alex stared in wonder. She was looking at a canal dug by hand through a thick forest about 1400 years before. It was wide; she'd read it might have been up to twenty feet, and about three feet deep.

"How much do you know about this here marvel? I don't want to bore you by telling you something you already know."

"Some. I found a few articles. But please, tell me everything. You know more than anyone else about this canal, since you're the reason it's being preserved."

Jacob beamed, pride emanating from every pore, wrinkle, and sun-caused freckle. He adjusted his cap, pulling it off his head and tugging it back on. He walked to the canal and sat down, his legs dangling over the edge, and motioned Alex to join him. "I'm not from here. 'Bama born and bred, but further north. This area's going gangbusters with all the tourists, thanks to folks like you," he said, tipping his cap to her. "Thought I'd dabble in some real estate. As I was scouting around, gettin' the lay of the land, I came across this sign that said 'Indian Ditch.' Now, what's that? I asked myself. Pulled over like I was driving an oval and needed a pit stop. I hadn't walked five feet when this tiny old lady came out of the woods. Scared the heck outta me, not the least because I was staring straight down the barrel of a shotgun."

Alex laughed, picturing a scene out of the Hatfield and McCoys legends.

"I swear if she'd stood that gun on end, it'd be as tall as her, that's how tiny she was. This was her land, she said, and I better get the H-E-double-hockey-sticks off." He chuckled, shaking his head at the memory.

"What did you do?"

"Now, I do pride myself on having a little bit of charm, being a southern boy and raised right by my Mama and Meemaw, but that woman nearly sent me back to my truck for a new pair of jeans, pardon the expression. Instead, I sucked it up and apologized, then launched into this long-winded tale of how I found arrowheads when I was just a tyke and my cousins stole them from me. By the time I took a breath, I'd worn the poor woman down. She put her gun under her arm, turned around and walked back into the woods. I stood there, like a darn fool, until she shouted back at me, 'You comin' or what? I ain't got all day.' I'm not one to keep a lady waiting, so you better believe I hightailed it after her. What I saw, well, it boggled the mind."

Jacob paused, a beatific smile taking years off his face as he recalled his encounter with the crotchety woman and his first glimpse of the "Indian ditch." Alex had been watching him as he talked. Now she swept her eyes over the ancient canal in the middle of a thick forest, marveling at the incredible feat of engineering. *They must have needed it for something important to put in that much effort*, she thought. "What did they use it for?" Alex asked.

"Transportation and trade, most likely. That's the going theory. This area, this whole hemisphere, actually, was a lot more populated than some people would have you believe. Folks used to think nobody lived around here more than a few months a year. Come to find out, even back in the seventh century, people stayed year round. If you're still here next week, I can show you the site of one of their villages."

Jacob's voice had taken on a tone of reverence, his *aw shucks* demeanor replaced with an aura of awe and respect.

"I'd love that," Alex said. "I'd planned to stay for at least another ten days." *Or longer, if they didn't quickly find out who killed Dr. Baker.*

"You just let me know. It's nice to meet someone who appreciates the complexity of the past. Unlike some around here," he muttered.

Alex gambled. "Like a certain couple of Doctors?"

Jacob grunted. "Make that three. Not to speak ill of the dead—oh yes, I heard about Harold, but those three wouldn't know a significant find if somebody pointed to it with a neon sign. So wrapped up in their *Conquistadors*," he sneered.

Alex placed her hands on the ground on either side of her knees and leaned forward to look closer at the ditch. The walls of the canal were precise. How many hundreds and thousands, maybe hundreds of thousands, had loaded their shallow-draft canoes with trade goods and floated down the waterway? She could barely contain her excitement about seeing the village of those who had most likely excavated it, and who would have greeted anyone who skipped the treacherous waters of the Gulf and instead used their faster, safer route.

But not yet. LuEllen had already texted Alex six times before she'd put her phone on silent when she arrived to meet Jacob. Cassidy had sent her a cryptic message saying only *3 poss. Elsie on warpath. Call at 10*. Alex hadn't heard from William yet, but she knew he was still getting his beauty rest. That man could sleep more than anyone she knew, which always confused her, not only because she was an unapologetic morning person, but also because he was so active.

"Will you be at the opening tonight?" Alex ventured.

Jacob snorted. "Wouldn't be caught dead at that sham. That medallion's no more real than my Aunt Mable's teeth. Don't look so surprised, young lady. There are older people than me around." He swung his legs under him and stood nimbly, then reached his hand out to help Alex up. They looked down into the canal. "I suppose you'll be there."

Alex nodded. "Dr. Sterling practically insisted I go, and she's not someone I want to upset."

"Wise."

"Why did you say it's a sham?"

"Because I know that dig site. There was never any village there, and there certainly were never any Spaniards. And de Soto? That barbarian never got near here, thank the good Lord. Not that it matters much to some. Soon as I heard Harold was having some big to-do proving Hernando'd set his jackboots on this soil, I knew he was back to his old ways." Jacob shook his head. "What Lu saw in him, I'll never know."

Alex cleared her throat. "Dr. Sterling showed me the site yesterday. And guess what? I found a chevron bead."

Jacob threw his head back and laughed, a long hearty cackle. "Oh, that's rich. Did you buy it? What she was selling you?"

"Nope," Alex smiled. "Not for one second."

He chortled. "Smart girl. Woman, I mean. Smart woman. Whelp, I suppose you've got better things to do than to hang out with an old fart like me. Let's get you back so you can get on with your day. And I'm serious about showing you that village. You just let me know when and I'll show you an authentic piece of history, one that tells a real story instead of lies and wishful thinking."

He turned away from the canal and led Alex back towards their cars, silent. When they reached his truck, he leaned against it, crossing his arms over his chest. "I heard Elsie Monroe caught Harold's case." Alex nodded. He sighed and studied his boots, then looked up at her. "Cassidy's in her sights then, I'm guessing. Tell you what. Elsie's partner, that Washington fellow, he's a good one and he owes me a favor. Elsie'll have her blinders on; I'm surprised Cass isn't already behind bars."

Alex tilted her head. "I thought you weren't from here?" she asked playfully.

"Not born and bred, but I've been here since Lu came back to raise that girl. I knew their parents," he said softly. "Now that was a tragedy." He stopped, interrupted by a vibrating phone. "That's my cue. As I was saying, Washington's good. I bet, if I asked him nicely, he'd meet you for some smoked tuna dip and a conversation about people who might have thought it was Harold's time to go."

"I'd appreciate that," Alex said.

"Consider it done, young lady." Jacob's thumbs tapped rapidly on his screen. "Done. I bet you'll get a text from Darrell before you pull out of this here lot."

"That must be some favor he owes you."

Jacob winked, climbed into his truck, closed the door, and drove away.

Chapter 14

Alex knocked lightly on Bessie's side door. "Rise and shine!" she called in a sing-song voice. William slowly opened the door, peering through the crack. His thick hair stood straight up on one side, the other side plastered flat against his skull. His shoulders slumped. He raised one finger and closed the door. Alex was too keyed up to sit, so she circled the campsite. She'd reached her eighth circuit by the time her friend emerged.

"At least you waited 'til a decent-ish hour." He passed her a mug of steaming coffee and sat down in one of the camp chairs, lifting his own to his lips and blowing on the surface. She waited, knowing he needed at least one sip before she could fill him in on her busy morning. He swallowed, closed his eyes briefly, and braced himself. "Alright. I'm ready now. Bring it on."

"How do you feel about smoked tuna dip?"

William cocked his head at her. "For breakfast? Seems like an odd choice, but I'm game."

She grinned. "Lunch, goof. We're meeting Detective Washington, and apparently he's obsessed with smoked tuna dip."

He coughed, snorting coffee out of his nose. "How'd you swing that?"

"I have my ways," she teased, then filled him in on her morning with Jacob Rex. The amateur archaeologist had been correct; the detective sent her a text message before she'd pulled out of the lot. After confirming with him, she finally read the messages from LuEllen. She had sent four more while Alex talked with Jacob. Each one contained a different theory about who could have killed Harold, and how Cassidy absolutely could not have done it, and how "that darn Elsie" was after her Cass. Alex sent a quick message letting her know she was on it, and replied to Cassidy's message, asking if things were OK and confirming she'd call at ten. She also asked for the location of the dig site where they'd found the medallion, and Cassidy responded with a map.

"Elsie's on the warpath, eh?" William asked after Alex told him about the message. "What's that mean?"

Alex checked her watch. "We'll know in about thirty minutes. Before I forget, I found out why she's got it out for Cassidy."

"Way to bury the lede. What did our golden child do to earn the never-ending ire of our dark-haired detective?"

Alex got up and crossed to her Subaru, grabbing her laptop from the front seat. "You finish your morning ablutions. I'm going to see if I can find out who their mysterious client was. I'll tell you what I learned about Detective Monroe when we're on the way to see her partner."

"Fine," William yawned. "Keep me in suspense." He walked over to Alex and kissed her on the cheek, then disappeared inside Bessie. She could hear his water tank kick in as she searched for ownership records for the land where Cassidy and Reid found the original medallion. When he emerged twenty minutes later, she'd removed at least one potential suspect for Dr. Baker's murder.

"I found the client," she said, "and he has been nowhere near Gulf Shores."

"Enlighten me, Ms. Drew. How could you find him when Cassidy and Reid could not?"

"As I said, I have my ways," she grinned. One of Alex's greatest pleasures was using her investigative skills, a talent she'd honed during her years as a reporter. "First of all, the dig site was in Guatemala."

"Hmm. And that's where Cassidy and Reid have been. So when Reid said they're still searching, sounds like he really meant they're still searching, as in present tense."

"Yep. Although there's a lot to search for in that country. Anyway, the land was registered to a corporation, of course, which was owned by another corporation and another, and another. I'm betting that's who signed their contract. One of those corporations. The thing about corporations, though, is they often have public records." She tapped the screen. "I found one name on every link of this chain. A billionaire famous for his reclusiveness and demands for privacy."

"So how do you know he couldn't have been here?"

"He died last year. There was an estate sale, which advertised 'unique items of considerable historical significance.' That," she said, pointing her index finger for emphasis, "is most likely how Vanessa and Gerald got the medallion. They bought it."

"Any of our oh-so-questionable antiquities dealers attend said auction?"

"I haven't been able to find that out. Yet." She checked her watch. "Time to call Cassidy."

Static filled the line. "Hello?" Alex called. "Cass? I can barely hear you." A door closed and the noise disappeared. "That's better. Where are you?"

"I'd rather not say. You know how I mentioned Elsie's on the warpath? She came looking for us at Lu's this morning. Fortunately, we got a motel last night. We're staying mobile today. If she can't find me, she can't arrest me."

"That explains LuEllen's barrage of texts this morning."

"Yeah, sorry about that. Anyway, I mentioned we've got three possibilities for the antiquities dealers who might have sold the replica."

"Were they some of the names you recognized?"

"Yep. Since I sent that text, we've ruled out two, and I'm ninety-nine percent certain the last candidate fits the bill. He's got a gallery in Miami and is respected for his, ahem, thoroughly researched provenance. He seems on the up-and-up, but we've had some dealings with him and know better. What about you?"

Alex filled her in on what she'd discovered about their former client, and about his death.

"That explains how the replica ended up on the market. Our dealer must have purchased it in the estate sale, then decided to resell it, with a twist." Alex heard a muffled voice in the background. "What? No. I'll ask," Cassidy said, then spoke into the phone again. "When did he die?"

"About nine months ago."

Alex could practically hear Cassidy nodding. "Timing fits. They'd need a couple months to get the estate in order, and another month or so to arrange the auction. It would take the last several months to create that whole dig site."

"And it is a fake," Alex confirmed, then told her about what Jacob had said that morning. "Why don't you email me the details on that last dealer and I'll see what else I can find out. Oh, and you may not have to be in hiding for long. We're meeting Detective Washington soon–alone."

"How'd you manage that?"

"Jacob. Apparently, Detective Washington owed him a pretty big favor."

"And we're collecting," William piped in.

"I do have one more question," Cassidy asked. "What was his name? The client?"

"Thornhill. Rupert Thornhill."

Cassidy audibly sighed. "I should have known," she breathed. "I should have known."

Alex arranged to contact Cassidy after their meeting with the police detective and hung up. She checked her email. Cassidy had already sent the information about the dealer. Gregory Talbot. Alex recognized the name; it had been near the top of Harold's list and was one of several he'd notated with a checkmark. A quick search pulled up article after article featuring his gallery, *Elusives*. He looked to be in his mid-sixties and had that polished skin attainable only by rigorous attention. She glanced at William, and thought, for probably the thousandth time, that she should start following his daily routine. The man had more skincare products in his travel bag than she had in her entire condo. She imagined Mr. Talbot's bathroom looked similar. In every photo, the gallery owner wore finely tailored suits, open-necked shirts, and colorful pocket squares. She guessed each item was custom made.

One of the earliest articles highlighted the ribbon-cutting at his exclusive gallery. Miami and Florida dignitaries, including the mayor and governor, flanked him as he held giant gold scissors. The building exuded Old World charm, with an ivory facade and faux cast-iron balconies. *Those aren't the only things that are fake,*

Alex thought. No name adorned the building. It was a place you knew about, or you didn't. Gregory Talbot was definitely a man of both means and connections.

"He's the one selling stolen goods? Just goes to show, you can't judge a book by his leather loafers," William said. "Think he's a suspect?"

Alex considered the distinguished-looking gentleman. Even in two-dimensional photos, he exuded an air of entitlement and confidence. This was a man untouched by concerns about money. This was a man used to getting what he wanted. This was a man, she thought, who wouldn't take kindly to any threats to his secure world. If Harold had called Talbot asking about the authenticity of the medallion, how would the dealer have reacted?

"Definitely."

Chapter 15

Alex pulled into a parking space but stayed in her seat. They were early for their meeting with Detective Washington, and she wanted to fill William in on what Zoe had told her about her mother.

"Wait a minute. Back up. Zoe, sculptor-of-shrimp-in-sand Zoe, is Detective Monroe's daughter?"

"Yep. The local paper covered a lot of stories about this county fair Zoe mentioned. In the articles leading up to it, everyone expected Elsie Monroe to be the star. She'd taken tap dance lessons since she was three, and although she was only six, her teacher thought she was a natural, and was a shoo-in for the top prize in her age group."

"Shoe-in. Tap dancer. Ha!"

"I also found an article about LuEllen's and Cassidy's parents," Alex continued, ignoring him. Mr. and Mrs. Devereaux, Alex explained, had been out for the evening, a rare occurrence, when a driver flew through a red light, totaling their car. It was a hit and run, and the culprit was never caught. The town rallied around young Cassidy. Over the next several weeks, article after article followed the golden-haired child, likening her to Shirley Temple with her adorable dimple. They lauded LuEllen, who'd made the ultimate sacrifice by giving up her promising career to come back and take care of her sister.

"So why would that make Elsie hate her?"

"Cassidy entered the talent show. They were in the same age group, of course. She read a poem. And she won."

William emitted a low whistle. "That's an awfully long time to hold a grudge. It seems a bit extreme to be that angry for that long over a talent show."

"Exactly what I thought. Nearly four decades? That's some pent up resentment right there. Then again, we're adults with adult emotions."

"One of us is," William grinned.

Alex smiled back. "True. But when you're six..." She lowered the windows to get some fresh air. "I had found the records for Cassidy and Reid's mystery client pretty quickly, and since you were still going through your beauty routine–" William preened, "–I thought I'd see if I could find out any more about what happened with Detective Monroe. Zoe said her grandfather was in and out of trouble, so I checked court records for any Monroes." Many municipalities had digitized their records. Baldwin County's didn't go back that far, but the local newspapers did. "I kept seeing references to a man named Jackson Monroe. Seems he spent most of the '80s and early '90s in jail, usually for crimes involving drugs and petty theft, but he also had a few big ones, including Grand Theft Auto.

"Jackson Monroe. Elsie's father?"

"That's what I'm guessing."

"Still doesn't explain why she'd be so mean to Cassidy, and for so long. It's been decades."

"When Elsie was a senior in high school, somebody stabbed Jackson and he died in the prison hospital. Right before her graduation. And Elsie was pregnant. Also, of probable importance, is that Cassidy was prom queen. "

"Oh wow. One teen is about to become a mom and her dad's murdered in jail, and the other's everybody's darling. What a sad story for Elsie. It seems like she's turned her life around, though."

"I agree, but if she had a very different image of what her life should have been, and she lost it because of bad timing while seeing another child get, from her perspective, preferential treatment, it could have a big impact."

"And apparently did." William mulled it over. "Here she is with her own sad childhood through no fault of her own, but there's no community rallying around her. It had to seem incredibly unfair. I'm wondering... do you think if Cassidy apologized, it would make a difference?"

Alex shrugged. "Maybe. I kind of doubt she'd be willing to. None of it's her fault. She did lose her parents, after all."

"Yeah, Cassidy's got her own reasons for resentment. Too bad they never found out who did it. I know closure's an illusion, but living your whole life knowing your parents' killer got away, even if it wasn't intentional, has to cause some serious damage." William looked out the window. Alex guessed he was thinking about his own parents. They'd been estranged for years, but recently had begun trying to repair their relationship. Alex was lucky; both her parents were alive, and they'd always been close. Almost always. They weren't very happy with her when she quit her newspaper career to be a travel writer, but they got over it.

Alex checked the time. "We've still got a few minutes, but why don't we go on in? We can have that smoked tuna dip waiting for him." They entered the restaurant, a cavernous space with a raised bar area and a stage off to the side. A chalkboard listed the specials and the bands who'd be playing that week. Once they sat at a table, they ordered a couple of sweet teas—real ones this time, not LuEllen's version—and the appetizer. The server had just placed the basket on the table when William gave a sigh of appreciation.

Alex looked up to see Detective Washington approaching their table. They stood up and shook hands with him. Hers practically disappeared in his grip.

They sat. The detective gestured to the basket filled with crackers and a mound of dip. "Jacob told you the way to my heart, didn't he now?" He tore the wrapper from a package of saltines and liberally spread the smoked tuna. "I could eat this every day and twice on Sunday."

Alex prepared her own cracker, but spoke before taking a bite. "We appreciate your meeting us."

"Absolutely," William said, covering his mouth so he wouldn't spray crumbs on the table. "I'm surprised you could get away from your partner."

Washington chuckled, a deep vibration. "Elsie—Detective Monroe—may come on strong, but she's good at what she does. She's got leads to follow, and so do I."

"Forgive me for saying so, but it seems like the only leads she's following lead directly to Cassidy."

The detective didn't take the bait. Instead, he opened another package of crackers. "Jacob mentioned you had information for me. Care to share? This isn't a social visit, even if it does involve this," he said, gesturing to the quickly emptying basket.

William and Alex eyed each other, silently agreeing Alex would be the one to lead the conversation. "While we know Cassidy couldn't have killed Dr. Baker, since we were with her from the moment we walked into the museum—"

"Except for when she went to confront him, I understand."

"She did, yes, but she wasn't gone long enough to poison him. Besides, I saw her racing down the hall. She didn't enter that courtyard, or even touch the basket with Simon's hazmat suit." The detective didn't respond. He reached for the last packet of saltines, opened them, spread dip on them, and put one in his mouth, maintaining eye contact the entire time. "But you know that. Right," Alex said. The man made her nervous.

William stepped into the gap left by Alex's uncharacteristic uncertainty. "We believe, and think it will be easy to prove, that Dr. Sterling and Dr. Price had means, motive, and opportunity."

Detective Washington rolled his eyes, then gestured for him to continue. William looked at Alex, who'd quickly recovered her confidence. "You may have heard the medallion is a fake," she said.

"Allegedly."

"It's definitely a fake. Anyway, Vanessa took me to the dig site, and to me it looked real, but Jacob told me that's impossible." She continued to tell him what the amateur archaeologist had told her that morning, that there were never any villages where the doctors had claimed to find the medallion.

"Jacob's a good man, probably the best man I know, but archaeology is his hobby, not his career. Plus, he's got a blind spot when it comes to anything related to the Spaniards. Or the French. According to him, they could do no right, and the natives could do no wrong. Absolutes are never true," he said with a deadpan expression on his face.

William guffawed. "Ha! I see what you did there."

The detective stood up, reached into his back pocket, extracted a ten from his wallet, and threw it on the table. "Thank you for the break, but I've got to get back to work. While I'm sitting here eating and chatting, there's a murderer on the loose."

Alex jumped out of her chair. "Wait!" she pleaded. "There's more."

He frowned, then slowly sat back down. "Go on, but make it fast."

Alex took a deep breath, then launched into the full story: what they'd learned about the original medallion, about the billionaire who'd funded Cassidy and Reid's excavation, and about his death and the ensuing estate sale. She told him about Gregory Talbot and his reputation for forged antiquities and their accompanying provenances that went beyond his success catering to elite collectors. As she explained her theory that Vanessa and Gerald had purchased the medallion at an illicit auction, most likely hosted by Talbot, the detective leaned back in his chair and crossed his arms. "If nothing else, those two make more viable suspects than Cassidy. Vanessa was with Dr. Baker when we arrived at the museum yesterday morning," she finished.

"Might be a good idea to find out where Mr. Talbot was, too," William suggested.

Detective Washington scowled at him, then turned back to Alex. "OK. Continue the story. What would be her motive?"

Alex focused on William. He wiped his mouth with a napkin. "We think Dr. Baker found out the medallion was fake and he confronted Vanessa. Simon mentioned this artifact was supposed to be his father's redemption, and that's kind of hard to do if it's based on lies."

"Why wouldn't Cassidy and Reid have told us yesterday the medallion was a forgery?"

"They couldn't." Alex explained about the contract the two had signed, preventing them from telling anyone. "They didn't know until this morning their client had died last year."

"Sounds like even more motive to kill Dr. Baker, if they thought he knew it wasn't real and planned to have the exhibit anyway."

Alex slumped. "That's a pretty weak motive. Besides, he didn't know. Cassidy never got the chance to ask him about it. He was dead when she got to his office."

"So she says." Detective Washington narrowed his eyes in thought, then unwrapped his arms, leaned forward, and stood up. "Gregory Talbot in Miami, right? I will check it out and fill Detective Monroe in on everything you've told me. But a word of advice? If you talk to Cassidy and Reid, tell them to stop hiding. It's only making things worse."

He walked away, stopping on his way out to say hello to every staff member he encountered. "He knows everybody," William said. "He really does come here all the time."

Alex stared off into the distance. "It doesn't seem like Cassidy's off the hook."

"He did say he'd look into Talbot."

"I'm not planning to wait for him. Nor am I giving Cassidy and Reid the all-clear, not while Detective Monroe's still focused on them." She stood up and they walked out of the restaurant.

"I noticed you didn't say anything about Elsie's past."

"It seemed too personal. It feels like something I should talk to her about."

William kissed her on the cheek. "This is why I love you."

Alex grinned. "Let's go see a man about a nefarious antiquities forger."

"You've got a man?"

"Figure of speech. But I'm guessing Cassidy and Reid do."

"Smart thinking. Lead the way."

Alex pulled into yet another small unpaved lot. It was the third in two days. The first had led to Vanessa and Gerald's bogus dig. The second, to the authentic, and remarkable, ancient canal. This time, the lot was at a national wildlife refuge. When she sent a text to Cassidy saying they needed to meet, the woman replied with another cryptic message. *It's all B.S. Ask Lu.* With a frustrated sigh, Alex had called LuEllen. The older sister laughed, the raucous sounds of a beachside restaurant on a gorgeous day in the background. "Bon Secour," she said, explaining her younger sister's shorthand. "That's basically our local Makeout Point. Cass got busted there a few times. *Too much cumin!"* LuEllen shouted. She must have covered the mouthpiece because the sound was muffled. She spoke directly into the phone again. "Funny she's still using it for her illicit rendezvous. I heard you had a tete-a-tete with Darrell?"

"Detective Washington? Yes. Sort of. He doesn't seem much better than Detective Monroe."

"Oh, don't let his stoic demeanor fool you. He's got heart. Much more than that darn Elsie. *Perfect. Now repeat that nineteen more times. Good job, young man."* Alex could hear LuEllen clapping before she returned to the phone. "Sorry about that. We're train-ing a new line cook and he gets a little carried away with the spices. Cass is asking you to meet her at the wildlife refuge and she's trying to be all secret agent woman. She's got to know that's the first place Elsie will look."

"Which is probably why she chose it. Hoping Elsie will also think it's too obvious."

"Good point. So," LuEllen said, lowering her voice. Alex could picture her cupping her hand around her mouth to keep anyone from hearing, even though she'd already said the important thing—where Cassidy would meet her—without any filter. "How's it looking?"

Alex had answered as truthfully as she could, which meant she hadn't given the older woman much comfort.

Chapter 16

G ravel pinged the underside of her Outback as Alex pulled up next to the bright blue F150. The cab was empty. Cassidy and Reid were probably waiting for them at the lagoon. Alex and William got out and began walking a well-manicured path. It curved through cypress trees and marsh grasses, leading them to a boardwalk. The canopy cleared and Alex saw the couple sitting on a bench facing the water. A loud caw, sounding almost prehistoric, caught her attention. She looked up to see a heron flying overhead. It descended and picked its way along the shoreline, its motions as fluid as a ballerina. She stopped to take in the scene, closing her eyes for a moment to savor the feel of the sun on her face. When she opened her eyes, it was to see Reid put his arm around Cassidy; she rested her head on his shoulder. They seemed to meld into one, and Alex wanted to turn around and leave them to this peaceful moment, but she knew they didn't have the luxury of time. The museum opening was in a few short hours and they needed answers.

As Alex and William neared, the couple heard them approaching and turned in unison. Once again, Alex thought how physically perfect they seemed, both individually and as a unit. Cassidy smiled. "I see you've found our safe harbor."

William smacked his forehead. "Bon Secour. French for *safe harbor*. Aren't you clever."

"Sorry to be so cloak and dagger, but I'd rather not be arrested."

Alex paused and studied her. "It must be hard to have someone dislike you so much."

"Especially when you're as delightful as you are."

Cassidy smiled at William, then spoke to Alex. "She's never liked me, for as long as I can remember. She even made fun of me for not having any parents."

William gasped. "That is *awful*. What a terrible person!"

"In her defense, she was only six, and you know kids have no filter. Sometimes that comes out as cruelty."

"Darlin', color it how you want, but that *is* cruel, and even a first grader should know that." William shook his head. He gave Alex an intense look. She knew he was trying to telepathically convince her to tell Cassidy why Elsie had always been so cruel.

"OK, OK. I'll tell them," Alex said. Cassidy listened, expressions of dismay, shock, and sorrow crossing her face as she learned the reasons for the detective's animosity.

"I had no idea," Cassidy said. "I was so caught up in my own grief. I was five!" she cried.

Reid soothed her, rubbing her back softly. "You couldn't have known, Cass. None of what Elsie went through is your fault. None of what *you* went through is your fault." Cassidy turned to him and sobbed, a deep, wrenching cry that tore at Alex's heart. She looked away, and saw that William also had tears in his eyes.

"I'm sorry," Alex murmured.

Cassidy sniffled, shaking her head. "It's better to know." She pulled her sleeve over her hand and wiped her nose, then walked over to the lagoon, bending over to rinse the fabric. "OK then. So what you're saying is we have to be the ones to figure out who killed Harold, because Elsie won't."

"I take it Detective Washington wasn't much help?" Reid asked.

Alex shrugged. "Maybe. We told him about the medallion's real history and he basically took it under advisement. He also said you two should stop hiding."

Cassidy shook her head vigorously. "Nope. No way. First time Elsie will know where I'm at is if she comes to the opening tonight. I won't be dragged in in secret, and that's exactly what she'd try to do. She thinks I'm the golden child? Then she can arrest me in front of the whole town, see how they react."

"Well, you are pretty golden," Reid said with a smile.

"Literally," William interjected. "I mean, not literally, because you're not made of gold, but look at you. Flawless. Not a child, but still golden."

Cassidy smiled, a small acknowledgement of his compliment. She kicked off her shoes and walked to the shore and into the water. The heron slowly tilted its head and eyed her, then flew off, water dripping from its feet.

Reid studied her. "We did find out something that should help." He walked over to Cassidy and pulled her phone out of her back pocket, then opened a PDF and handed the device to Alex. "That's the auction listing for the medallion."

"How'd you get that?" Alex asked.

Cassidy turned around and joined them. "I know someone who receives invitations to underground auctions." When Alex raised an eyebrow, she explained. "College roommate. We went different directions. Hers led her more towards the underbelly. It's a long story."

"Normally I'd say we've got time, but we don't." Alex read the listing, then texted it to herself.

"Why isn't there a picture of the medallion? People really buy these kinds of things sight unseen?" William asked.

Cassidy shook her head. "The description narrows down who's serious. Then the potential bidder contacts the seller. After a deposit—a significant deposit—is put down, then they get to see what it looks like. But that description fits our medallion."

"Still risky, isn't it?" Alex asked. "To buy an artifact and then make up some whopper about digging it up yourself? Even being so bold as to have a very public event and inviting journalists to the dig site?"

"Not really. The kinds of people who have access to these kinds of auctions aren't exactly going to publicize it when one of their colleagues decides to make the most out of it. And that's how they'd see it, as an opportunity cleverly capitalized upon," Reid explained.

"Besides," Cassidy continued, "people buy big lies because they're audacious enough they must be true. This is the height of arrogance, and that says Vanessa and Gerald all over."

"I wonder if it'll be enough. If we send the listing to Detective Washington, I mean," Alex pondered.

Before she'd finished speaking, Cassidy and Reid were both shaking their heads. "We need more. We need a confession," Cassidy said.

Alex frowned. "Yes, you probably do."

William consulted his phone to check the time. "We've still got a few hours before the opening. What do you need us to do?"

Reid reached into his pocket and pulled out his keys. "How would you feel about switching vehicles with us? Elsie'll be on the lookout for our truck, and we're more likely to blend in with yours. There are about a gazillion Outbacks around here."

"Give or take a few," William agreed.

Alex reached for their keys, exchanging hers at the same time. "Guess we're in it now," she grinned. "Would this be considered obstructing an investigation?"

"Consider it helping a friend," Cassidy smiled warmly. "Thank you. I don't think I've said that yet. Thank you for everything you're doing to help us."

Alex returned the smile, and William spoke. "My beautiful friend here has a finely tuned sense of right and wrong, and what Elsie's trying to do to you is wrong."

"There's a lot wrong with this whole situation, especially Dr. Baker's murder," Reid said. "We may have had our issues with him, but we wouldn't wish death on anyone."

"Almost anyone. I can think of a couple..."

"Now, now, I know you don't mean that, no matter how much you don't like Vanessa and Gerald."

"Think of all the damage they've done, not just to us, but to everything we stand for." Cassidy scrunched her lips together, then exhaled. "But yes, you're right. Not even those two deserve murder. They do, however, deserve to be behind bars."

"Let's see if we can make that happen."

Chapter 17

Alex reached for the grab handle and pulled herself into the cabin of the truck.

"Oof, this thing is tall," William remarked. "If they wanted to drive LuEllen anywhere, they'd have to give her a stepstool."

"More like a ladder." She pushed the ignition. "Electric vehicles freak me out. They're so quiet."

"Did I tell you I'm thinking of getting one? A hybrid, anyway?"

Alex turned to him in surprise as she pulled out of the lot. "What about Bessie?"

"I adore Bessie, but she's not the most fuel efficient thing in the world. It's probably a long way off anyway. I can't take the chance I'll be stuck in the middle of nowhere with no charging stations in sight."

"And you are often in the middle of nowhere."

"That I am. Speaking of, can I see the map of billionaire boogeyman's dig site?"

Alex pulled her phone out of its holder. They stopped at a red light and she pulled up her text messages. She was just handing the phone to him when she heard a chirp. She looked up and saw flashing red and blue lights in her rearview mirror. "Crap. Looks like they're pretty serious about hands-free driving around here."

William turned to look behind them as Alex pulled over. "I don't think it's that."

Alex checked her side-view mirror and saw Detective Monroe cautiously approaching. The police officer reached to her side and drew her gun, holding it with both hands as she neared the driver's side door. Alex swallowed, lowered the windows, and put both hands on the steering wheel. Through her peripheral vision, she saw William put his hands on the dashboard. He was watching Detective Washington approach from the other side. Alex saw the flash of irritation cross Monroe's face when she realized who was driving.

"You," Detective Monroe spat. She removed her mirrored sunglasses and put them on the top of her wiry curls. The look she gave Alex was pure frustration. "What are you doing in this vehicle?"

William leaned forward, leaving his hands where both officers could see them. "I'm thinking of getting an electric or a hybrid," he explained. "Cassidy and Reid let us borrow this to see if I'd like it."

Detective Monroe narrowed her eyes, then focused on her partner, who was leaning against the passenger side and peering into the cab. "Are you buying this?"

"Nope," Detective Washington responded.

"No, seriously, we were just talking about it, weren't we?"

Alex nodded. "William is very environmentally conscious," she squeaked, then coughed. She hated it when she got meek around pushy people.

"Then why aren't you driving?" Monroe asked, returning her gaze to William.

"Because this thing has a massager. Look!" He reached towards the touchscreen to pull up the controls.

Detective Monroe waved him off, then sighed. Detective Washington had been watching his partner closely. He visibly relaxed as she put her gun back in its holster. "I should arrest you both for obstructing an investigation," she said. "Where are Cassidy and Reid?"

"We don't know."

"I'm serious. I can arrest you. Where are they?"

"We really don't know. They didn't tell us where they were going, or what they were doing. I do know they'll be at the opening tonight," Alex said.

Detective Monroe cocked her head. "They will, will they? Why are you telling me this?"

"Because we don't want to be arrested?" William ventured. "I would not do well in jail. Handcuffs, yes. Jail, no."

Alex gave him an exasperated glance. "Because Cassidy did not murder Dr. Baker. We even gave your partner proof."

"Oh yes, I saw this supposed listing. You're saying that *Doctor* Vanessa Sterling and *Doctor* Gerald Price bought their medallion at an underground auction, then created a whole excavation site and arranged a well-publicized event to show off this artifact. Then what, *Doctor* Harold Baker discovered this elaborate ruse, threatened to expose them, and *Doctor* Vanessa Sterling killed him? I thought you two were travel writers. I didn't think you wrote fiction." As she talked, the detective focused entirely on Alex, ignoring the traffic that was backing up because they'd taken over one of the lanes. People stared as they drove past, trying to figure out what kind of trouble the couple in the shiny new pickup truck had gotten into.

Alex returned her stare, thinking of her as Elsie, childhood nemesis to Cassidy, instead of as a detective. It was hard not to say anything about what she'd learned, but Alex was too frustrated and she knew she'd come across as cruel. "Yes, that's exactly what we're saying, because that's exactly what happened." She turned to speak to Detective Washington. "Did you check out that gallery owner we gave you?"

"Gregory Talbot? Of course I did. That's what we, who are detectives, do. We detect. We investigate."

"And we suggest you leave the detecting and investigating to us," Elsie said. She looked at her partner again before continuing. "We're going to let you go, for now. But my patience is very, very thin." She pulled a card out of her shirt pocket and handed it to Alex, waiting until she took it from her. "If you hear from Cassidy Devereaux and or Reid McKinley, you call me immediately. If you don't, and I hear you've been in contact with them, I may change my mind and arrest you anyway." She turned on her heel and walked back towards the Crown Vic, its flashing lights skipping as the detective crossed their path.

Detective Washington leaned in before also returning to the car. "Talbot was at an auction yesterday morning in Miami. A *legitimate* auction."

Alex nodded. "Thank you," she said. "And Vanessa? Are you looking into her?"

The policeman stood up and walked away. Alex waited for the police car to swing around her, then she slowly eased back into traffic.

"That was intense," William said. "That woman's really got it out for Cassidy."

Alex simmered while her heart rate slowly returned to normal. "Knowing why doesn't make it easier to swallow. Simon thought Cassidy had a vendetta against his father, but I don't think he had any idea what that really looks like."

"You know, she may be determined to pin this murder on her, but the evidence seems pretty thin."

"Almost nonexistent, if you ask me. I'm an eyewitness flat out telling her there's no way she had time to get the poison and then administer it to Harold."

"In her defense, eyewitnesses are notoriously unreliable."

"Unless you happen to be a trained observer. I may not work for a newspaper anymore, but I still have my journalistic skills," Alex complained.

"And darn fine skills they are. What do you think of their advice to leave detecting to the detectives?"

"Bunch of balderdash. We do that, and Cassidy's going to end up in jail. Nope. We need to look into it ourselves. Starting with Mr. Gregory Talbot."

"I thought he had an alibi."

"For the murder, yes, but he still sold fake goods, including a fictional history. I'm sure Vanessa and Gerald wouldn't be too thrilled to find out they'd bought a replica."

"What's the plan?"

"I'll let you know when I've come up with one."

Alex sat at the breakfast bar and typed rapidly on her laptop. She re-read the email, then hit send. She stood, stretched, and paced up and down, from the front door to the balcony and back, over and over as she waited for a reply. William sat outside, typing away on his own computer. They'd swung by Bessie to pick up his laptop on the way back to A & W HQ, as he'd dubbed the condo.

Her computer dinged. She'd gotten a response. Alex had reached out to a reporter friend who covered the arts scene, including galleries specializing in rare antiquities. She needed an introduction to Mr. Talbot. Her friend, Tad, had covered the Miami gallery's opening for Chicago's biggest arts magazine, and she'd asked him to contact the owner. Alex had partnered with Tad to cover Stanhope's trial, and they'd spent many hours going over details and strategies at Coda, Alex's favorite jazz and blues club. They hadn't seen each other much over the years, but Alex sent him cards for his wedding and the births of their now three children.

A -

Talbot's expecting your call. I told him you wanted to interview an expert regarding antiquities discovered in the American southeast, especially those with Spanish colonial ties, and he's the only one who came to mind, naturally. I explained it had to be today since you were on deadline. People like him love stuff like that. Makes them feel important, as you know oh so well.

Don't worry about burning this bridge. The man's a self-inflated peacock, and one of the privileges of being an award-winning (fluffing my own feathers) acerbic critic is he needs me more than I need him. I've given you the match. Light at will.

Gayle and the girls say hi. (Well, the oldest two say hi. Greta's vocabulary is still a bit limited, considering she's all of three months old.) Come over for dinner when you get back. It's been too long.

T

Alex smiled and walked out to the balcony to tell William she had an in. "It's good to know people," he said, swinging his legs off the table. "How are you going to play it?"

"By ear. I've got a broad outline, but you know how it goes. Ask, listen, and react." She walked back inside and inserted her earbuds.

Chapter 18

A lex stifled another yawn. *Self-inflated peacock* was an understatement. Talbot droned on while Alex made appropriate noises to let him know yes, she was still listening, and yes, he was still fascinating. While Talbot talked, she replied to Tad, informing him that after this conversation, he was going to owe *her* a favor, not the other way around. She'd asked two questions. The first: how Talbot got his start in the antiquities business. She meant this as a warm-up. She'd used a similar question countless times in countless interviews with countless entrepreneurs, even more so since she began travel writing than when she was an investigative journalist. In fact, she'd rarely asked anything so basic during her newspaper years. Those weren't the kinds of stories she wrote. But every time she did ask it, whether interviewing a hedge fund director indicted with fraud or the owner of a candy shoppe in a town with a population of 876, the interviewee would give her the Cliffs Notes version. Just the facts, ma'am. Five minutes. Ten minutes, tops.

Talbot? His beginnings were so auspicious they required thirty-two minutes. Probably longer, but Alex politely (or maybe not-so-politely) interrupted him to ask him her second question: why Spanish colonial antiquities?

That opened another extended monologue. It had now been forty-five minutes. If Alex didn't speed things up, they'd never make it to the opening that night, and she had more "detecting and investigating" to do. When Talbot completed his history lesson on the founding of St. Augustine and launched into de Soto's landing in what is now Tampa, Alex found her chance.

"It's funny you should mention de Soto," she said. "I'm attending an event tonight celebrating his exploration of the New World." She stuck her tongue out at William, who had come inside to witness her pacing during the never-ending call and was now mimicking a gagging reflex.

"Hmm. And where would that be?" Talbot's voice had been meticulously trained to sound like someone who'd attended private schools, boarding schools, finishing schools, Ivy League schools. The kind of person who played polo instead of field hockey, who knew the difference between Monet and Manet. But after nearly an hour of listening to him drone on, and on, and on, Alex heard the undercurrent of his upbringing. She hadn't called him blind. She'd found out as much as she could about him in the limited time she'd had, and what she'd discovered was that Gregory Talbot was really Diego Mendoza. He'd grown up in Mexico City, an orphan, bounced around shelters and foster homes. She would have admired him, and how he'd gone from squalor to become one of the most well-respected men in his field, if he'd done it with a modicum of integrity.

"The Gulf Coast History and Archaeology Museum. Have you heard of it?"

For once, Talbot was silent.

"I thought you might, because the focus of tonight's event is a medallion. *El Beso de la Muerta*, it's called. I saw it just yesterday morning and it's stunning. The artistry involved in creating this work of art, the delicateness of the gold filigree, the lustrous pearls, could only have been created in Spain, correct? I believe that's what the listing stated, or something along those lines. My source told me it was purchased through one of your auctions and was kind enough to share your description."

"*Merde*," he growled, then recovered with a cough. "I think you must be mistaken. I've never heard of an item that matches that description. It seems your source was incorrect." His carefully clipped tone was fully in place.

"I doubt it," Alex replied. "Dr. Vanessa Sterling—you're familiar with her, of course. Everyone in your field is, and she's been at your gallery multiple times. At least, according to the society pages," she chuckled. "She's been searching for something like this for some time, hasn't she? Proof that de Soto and his expedition went many, many more places than the history books would like for us to believe."

William gagged again. Alex winked at him. She was actually enjoying this, which slightly concerned her.

"Yes, of course I'm familiar with Dr. Sterling. She and her husband have made several important and impactful discoveries. Oh!" Talbot said, as if he just realized something. "You must be talking about Dr. Baker's museum, up in Gulf Shores. Yes, I'm aware of that incredible find. But I assure you, I know nothing of any auction. My understanding is that Drs. Sterling and Price discovered this medallion. They found it near Oyster Bay, if my memory serves me. Now, if you'll please excuse me, I need to get back to my gallery. We, too, are presenting important works this evening, and I must resume preparations. Good day."

Alex removed her earbuds and put them back in the case. She grinned at William. "That man definitely sold the medallion to Vanessa and Gerald."

"You got confirmation? You are amazing, my dear."

"Not quite. A case of *I think thee doth protest*, etc. He's rattled, though. I wouldn't be surprised if his first course of action was to call them."

"Well, you did imply she was your source." William looked at his watch. "Barnacles! I better get back and get ready for this evening."

His action prompted Alex to do the same. "We've got an hour before it starts, and I would like to be there at the beginning. Want to Lyft back to Bessie and I'll pick you up at 6:40? That should give you plenty of time to get ready."

"M'lady, you flatter me with your opinion of my speediness, but that ship has sailed. I'll do what I can in the short amount of time allotted to me." He eyed Alex, who wasn't petite, but also wasn't tall. "You're wearing a dress, aren't you? How are you going to get into, and out of, that truck without falling on your face? Forget I asked. I know you'll handle it with your customary grace."

"Yes, because I am so known for my gracefulness," she said, walking him to the door. He focused on his screen as he opened his ride-sharing app. "I'll see you in forty."

William groaned. "That's barely enough time to steam my tux. But for you, I'll race like a bunny."

Alex shook her head while closing the door behind him. She didn't have much time to get ready, either, but one of the benefits of having super-short hair was that it didn't require much preparation. There wasn't a lot she could do besides add a little product to control the curls, run a comb through it, and hope for the best.

After a quick shower and a fresh application of make-up, Alex padded in her bare feet and her robe back to the breakfast bar and awakened her laptop. She had just enough time to do some quick digging before she had to don her dress and leave to pick up William. Fortunately, the gown she traveled with didn't require any steaming. She'd learned the hard way, after one of her early press trips left her scrambling for evening wear, to pack at least one elegant outfit. Wrinkle-free, of course. Unlike William, who traveled with his home, she couldn't be bothered to pack a steamer with her everywhere she went.

Chapter 19

"Wow. Zer." William eyed Alex up and down, wiggling his eyebrows as he swept her body. He was the only man who could give her that sort of blatant appraisal without either making her feel uncomfortable or earning her anger.

"This ol' thing?" She grinned, smoothing the silky fabric against her skin. The full length black sheath dress featured a slit up her thigh, making it easy for her to move, and to get in and out of very large pickup trucks. "You've seen this at least half a dozen times."

"Yes, and you look even more dazzling each time you wear it. I love how you accessorize it. Those pops of color make it fresh and new, and oh, so very you."

Alex adjusted the sheer red scarf she'd draped around her neck, its long ends flowing behind her. She'd added chandelier earrings of faceted beads in a cascading rainbow of colors. Each bead shimmered as it caught the light, almost creating a prism effect. She appreciated William's compliments. He hadn't seen her wear the spaghetti-strapped dress since before her lumpectomy. To her, the different sizes of her breasts were obvious, as was the scar where her port had been inserted. She suddenly realized she no longer felt self-conscious about either. This was her body, her strong, survivor's body, and she loved it.

They drove to the museum, drawn by spotlights sweeping the sky. The valet agreed to park the truck where they could leave quickly if necessary. Alex claimed she had an early morning, which was why they'd arrived precisely on time, a little white lie to encourage the young man to give them an easily accessible spot. The early morning wasn't a fib; she always had early mornings, but the reason for arriving when the doors would open was. She knew she didn't need to volunteer an explanation to the valet, but Alex felt it was always good to be kind, to treat people like people, and that meant requesting, not demanding.

The valet escorted her around the front of the truck. William waited gallantly, his arm extended. She wrapped her fingers around his bicep and squeezed. "You, my friend, are some delicious eye candy."

He leaned down and kissed her on the top of her head. "As are you. Shall we?"

They entered the historic building. As planned, they were two of the first to arrive. The museum looked completely different than it had the day before. Decorators had transformed the wide hallway into an elegant reception area. Tall tables dressed in linens were arranged among statuesque palms and expansive ferns. Strings of muted lights criss-crossed the high ceilings. Candles flickered. A trio played chamber music. It hardly seemed like the same corridor they'd entered yesterday, the hallway Cassidy had traversed in her efforts to confront Dr. Baker, and then returned to deliver the horrible news of his death.

A tuxedoed server carrying a tray of champagne offered it to Alex and William. She released her friend's arm and he picked up two glasses. He handed one to her. "Cheers," they said, as they touched the crystal flutes to each other, and resumed walking towards the Beauregard Chalmers Exhibition Hall where the medallion was displayed. Its doors were closed, a podium with a microphone placed in front of them. Alex imagined Simon would give an impassioned speech in front of the thick cedar, followed by a dramatic flourish as the doors opened to reveal his father's last acquisition. Since learning the medallion was fake, she'd been plagued with the need to inform Simon of the artifact's true past. But she also needed to elicit a confession from Vanessa, and it seemed safest to do that while surrounded by people. As Alex and William strolled, she could think of only one way to ensure Dr. Sterling paid for what she'd done. Unfortunately, while Simon would learn who killed his father, that also meant he would learn the artifact was worthless in a way guaranteed to humiliate him.

The friends stopped occasionally to ostensibly admire the framed portraits of early explorers, including the one of de Soto, which had nearly gotten William's hand smacked the day before. "I wonder where Simon is?" Alex asked, scanning the growing crowd.

William searched also, but didn't see him either. "He's probably still arranging last-minute details. Dr. Baker did say he liked things to be just right."

"This is going to be difficult."

"When he finds out about the medallion, you mean?"

Alex sipped her champagne. "Yes. At least he'll know his father tried to do the right thing. Unfortunately, it got him killed."

"You seem pretty certain about what happened. Although I agree that what you suspect is the most obvious answer."

"What is?" A seductive alto whispered. They turned to see Vanessa, resplendent in a scarlet gown with a neckline that plunged to her navel. Multiple strands of pearls dangled from her neck, their varying lengths drawing attention to every part of her torso, the longest dangling below her waist. Behind her, Gerald adjusted the cuffs of his form-fitting tuxedo. Neither of their costumes, for there was no doubt in Alex's mind that this was a part the couple played, left much to the imagination.

"That tonight will be an unmitigated success," William said, lifting his glass to the couple. They eyed him warily, then delicately tapped their glasses to his and to Alex's.

"Of course it will be," Gerald said. "Our unveilings always are. This one in particular will be most gratifying." He focused on the portrait behind Alex and William. "You've chosen an excellent spot. Nuño de Guzmán is one of our favorites."

The two swept away as if they were at a royal ball and not a museum in Lower Alabama. "Unmitigated success for justice," William corrected. "I really do not like those two."

"Nor do I."

"Do you think Mr. Talbot informed the doctors of your little phone call this afternoon?"

Alex turned her back to the painting of the conquistador, considered one of the most brutal of all, and watched the couple as they floated from one cluster of guests to the next. She shook her head slowly. "I know I said I thought he would, but no. I don't think so. I think he'd want to keep any hint of exposure quiet. It'd be bad business if people thought his secret auctions weren't so secret. Besides, I don't think those two," Alex pointed her glass in the doctors' direction, "would have been so cordial."

William shivered. "Especially since their idea of cordial leaves something to be desired as it is. From what you told me about Mr. Talbot, you may need to watch your back, my dear. He sounds like he might be dangerous."

Alex patted her friend on the arm. "I'm a small fish. He's got an entire sea of bigger threats." She scanned the room. It was now socially acceptable to arrive, so the crowd had increased dramatically. Through the fluctuating currents of well-heeled men and women, she spotted a familiar face. "There's Detective Monroe now."

William searched, then focused as he located the police officer. "Would you look at her? She cleans up nicely."

That she does, Alex agreed. The detective was obviously working, wearing a black pantsuit and sensible shoes, but she'd left her hair down. Her riotous curls shone in the candlelight. A hush fell over the room. Everyone turned towards the marble stairs that led to the second floor galleries. Simon stood at the top, dressed in a full tuxedo with waistcoat, tails, pocket square, and bowtie, holding a brass-knobbed, brass-tipped cane. He even wore a cape and a top hat.

"Very *Phantom of the Opera*," William commented.

The botanist descended slowly, the tip of his cane tapping with each step. The sound rang out across the hushed room. Alex guessed they weren't the only ones who hadn't seen him in quite this light before. He stopped at the halfway point and adjusted his bowtie. His awkwardness had disappeared. In its place was confidence, even a touch of swagger. "Welcome," he called out in a resonant voice that let everyone know they were in his house. "Thank you for being here." Simon pulled out a pocket watch.

"He's got a *pocket watch*," William whispered, causing every table within a ten-foot radius to turn towards him and shush him. "A literal pocket watch."

Simon glanced in their direction, his eyes narrowing at the disturbance. "We've got a bit of time before the ceremonies begin.

Please, enjoy yourselves. I know it's what my father would have wanted."

Chapter 20

Simon paused dramatically, then continued down the stairs with slow, measured steps. He reached the bottom. Conversation gradually resumed. Alex followed his path through the room, which was easy to do since he was both tall and wore a stovepipe hat. Through a break in the crowd, she saw Simon call over a server. He gave him his cape and hat, but he held onto the cane.

"That seems like quite the affectation," Alex said.

"He wears it well, though, don't you think?"

Alex considered. "No. It's a costume. A part he's playing. Just like those two," she gestured with her nearly empty glass to Vanessa and Gerald. "Let's get another glass and move to the front. I want to try to catch Simon before he speaks, and he'll eventually end up there."

William extended his arm for her to take, but Alex couldn't hold it for long. The path to the temporary bar set up near the door to the courtyard was too narrow and they had to weave through scores of richly-attired guests. Alex wondered how many of them attended because they had an interest in antiquities, how many were there because it was the thing to do in their crowd, and how many were there to catch a glimpse of the grieving son. As they neared the bar, she noticed the basket where Simon had deposited his hazmat suit was gone. She tilted her head towards the space where it had been. "They must have taken the basket into evidence."

"Or they just moved it out of the way because of the event." William looked both ways, then opened the door. "Yep. It's right inside."

"Excuse me. What do you think you're doing?" Simon appeared beside them.

"My sincere apologies, Mr. Baker. I just had to get another peek at your garden. What you've grown here is quite remarkable."

Simon studied William, then spoke deliberately. "Yes, it is. That is the point. And that area is off-limits. I would think you, of all people considering what happened yesterday, would know that." He took a drink of his champagne, leaning casually on his cane and glaring at them. Alex was drawn to his hands, which were encased in black gloves. They looked to be made of leather, a supple hide that invited her to reach out and caress it. She stopped herself before actually doing so. Simon put the cane under his left arm, took her hand, and lifted it to his lips. The gloves felt like velvet. "You look stunning, Ms. Paige."

Who was this person? she wondered. It was like a body snatcher had switched the lanky, nervous man she'd met the day before and replaced him with a Rico Suave wannabe. *Has he been taking lessons from Gerald?* She gave him a small smile. "Thank you, Mr. Baker."

"Simon, please."

"Yes, of course. Thank you, Simon. This is quite the event."

He nodded. "It was all planned in advance. My father certainly knew how to throw a soiree. It's too bad he isn't here to see it." He stopped and stared into space, then shook his head. "But, he isn't, so I must carry on what he began. However," he leaned in, speaking quietly, "I have plans for this tired museum. Rather ingenious plans. I'd love to show them to you before you leave." He straightened, gave Alex a conspiratorial wink, and spun on his heel.

"Mr. Baker, Simon, I mean," Alex called. When he turned back, she put on her most charming smile. "I wondered if I could have a moment to speak with you before the unveiling?" When he frowned, she continued in a placating tone. "I realize you're very busy, but it's important. I promise you I wouldn't ask if it weren't."

Simon paused, drumming his fingers on the brass ball of his cane. "As you wish. Meet me here in fifteen minutes. 8:15? Good. I do hope you won't be wasting my time, especially this evening."

He turned on his heel and walked directly through the line of people waiting to get refills of their drinks. He held his cane by the shaft and tapped bare backs and tuxedoed shoulders alike with the brass topper as he made his way through the crowd. William rattled his head. "Body snatcher. I swear. If I didn't think it'd get me booted out of here, I'd be channeling my inner Donald Sutherland and pointing at whatever-that-is with my silent scream. That is *not* the Simon Baker we met yesterday morning."

"No, it is not," Alex agreed.

"Do you think it's wise to talk to him, especially to tell him he's about to make himself the laughingstock of the entire room, maybe of the whole archaeological community?"

"That's what I'm hoping to prevent. If he knows, he'll have to cancel it, right? Thank everyone for coming, consider it a memorial to his father, hope you enjoyed the party?" Alex sounded doubtful, even to herself. "Listen. Detectives Monroe and Washington are here. Vanessa and Gerald are here. We just need to get them to confess."

"And how do you plan to do that?" William asked.

"Yes, Ms. Paige. How *do* you plan to do that?"

Alex turned slowly towards the sultry voice behind her. She was really getting tired of people sneaking up on her. *Al Capone may have been a monster, but he was right about one thing: always keep your back to the wall,* she thought. "Do what?" she asked testily.

Vanessa scowled. She pulled Alex in for what would look to others like a hug, but as she did so, she gripped Alex's arm tightly. "Do not toy with me, Ms. Paige. You have no idea what I'm capable of."

Alex could feel the sharp tips of the doctor's nails digging into her flesh. She yanked her arm back. She'd had quite enough of this bully. "Oh yes. I'm perfectly aware of what you're capable of doing. Not the least of which is defrauding not only one man, but also his son, his entire community, and history in general."

Vanessa glared. She turned to her husband, who took her cue and growled at Alex. "What did we tell you about leaving this to the professionals? You don't know what you're talking about, and if you aren't careful—"

"You'll what?" William said, his charming persona replaced by his protective instincts. "Murder Alex? Just like you did Dr. Baker? Go ahead. You'll find your weapon of choice right through there," he said, gesturing to the door to the courtyard. "But you already know that, don't you, *Doctor* Sterling."

The crowd around them had quieted as the drama unfolded. At William's mention of Dr. Baker's murder, they began to whisper.

"I don't know what you're talking about," Vanessa hissed. "We did Harold a favor. We brought him the most significant find he could ever dream of. Gave it to him on a red carpet. This would have put him, and his little museum, on the map once and for all. He's been running this like a community center for two decades. If it weren't for us, this would be a run-down shack with a bunch of worthless trinkets. We brought him fame. We brought him redemption."

Alex stared. Redemption. The word kept surfacing. Thoughts bounced around in her mind and she wished, for once, instead of a disco ball, her brain would resemble an equation. A plus B equals there's your murderer. She couldn't get to it, though. *It can't still be chemo brain, can it?* she lamented. After months of fogginess and the seeming inability to pluck words when previously they'd been falling off the tree, she'd finally felt like her mind was back on track. But this, another death, another murder, and she felt like she was going to short-circuit.

No, she commanded herself. *It's there. Everything you need is right there, waiting for you to relax and figure it out.*

As Alex struggled with her thoughts, Vanessa's diatribe had taken on a muffled quality. The vapor lifted. Alex focused on the doctor, whose voice was clear again. "He chose anonymity. He chose to be small."

Another voice responded. Clear. Distinct. Succinct.

"He chose integrity."

The room of well-dressed, well-heeled guests turned as one to the entrance of the museum. Cassidy stood, framed by palm trees. She drew all the light in the room. Her dress shimmered, a deep bronze three tones darker than the color of her skin. Her golden hair danced in the glow from the strings of lights and flickering candles, and her hazel eyes bore into Vanessa as if she were drilling a hole into her mind. But none of that existed in comparison to the medallion Cassidy wore around her neck.

Chapter 21

"**Y**ou!"

The word echoed in surround sound as three people simultaneously shouted: Simon, who had nearly reached the exhibition hall; Vanessa, who stood with Gerald next to Alex and William; and Elsie. The detective was closest to the entrance. She pushed forward. "Cassidy Devereaux, you are under arrest for the murder of Dr. Harold Baker. Do not move."

The room collectively gasped. Heads swiveled from one woman to the other.

"I'm not going anywhere, Elsie." LuEllen and Reid appeared at Cassidy's side. They moved in front to block Elsie from getting too close, even crossing their arms across their chests to act as barricades. Alex thought it would have been sweet, especially seeing short LuEllen look her fiercest, if the situation weren't so dire. The room was silent, except for a shrill cackle.

"I knew it! I knew it was you. Little miss goodie two-shoes," Vanessa spat. It wasn't a figure of speech; Alex wiped saliva off the back of her neck and glared at the brunette.

"Is no one going to address the medallion in the room?" William whispered. As usual, everyone heard. They turned to stare at him.

Cassidy drew their attention back to her. She brought her hand up to her pendant and caressed it. "You mean this old thing?

Except it's not old, is it, Vanessa? Or authentic. In fact, it's about as authentic as the one in that hall." Cassidy pointed to the closed doors, in front of which Simon stood. Alex noticed he was smiling.

Detective Monroe continued to push her way towards Cassidy. "Let me through," she shouted. The police officer gradually got closer, but as she reached the last row of guests in front of her quarry, Detective Washington blocked her way. She tried to push past him, but he was like a wall. "Darrell, move. Right now."

"No, Elsie. We need—we *all* need to hear what Ms. Devereaux has to say." He waited. Detective Monroe clenched her fists so tightly her knuckles whitened. She rolled her neck, glared at her partner, and stepped back. "You were saying?" Detective Washington prompted.

Cassidy acknowledged him with a curt nod. "The medallion is a fake."

"Liar!" Vanessa shouted. "You're the fake!"

"The medallion is a fake," Cassidy repeated, "and so is its so-called legend. Those two *doctors*," she said the word with a derision so complete it felt slimy, "manufactured the entire story."

"How do you know?" someone asked. Alex couldn't see who.

"Because we found the original eleven years ago in Guatemala. This replica is lovely," Cassidy said, lifting the pendant, "but it's no more real than Dr. Sterling's...hair color." The room erupted in laughter. Vanessa tried to leap forward, but Gerald held her back. A pair of officers who'd entered with the detectives slowly circled the crowd, nearing the doctors.

"Where is the original?" Detective Washington asked.

"No one knows. It was stolen," Reid said. "Our client had a couple of replicas made because he didn't want anyone to know."

"Lies. It's all lies. Talbot promised us it was real," Vanessa cried.

Gerald closed his eyes and dropped his head. "You did not just say that, my dear. Do you realize what you've done?"

One of the officers reached Vanessa. He grabbed her wrists and pulled them behind her back. She wrestled with him. "Ow. Stop. You're hurting me."

"Vanessa, stop fighting. Just shut up, and stop fighting," Gerald commanded.

She scowled at her husband, but did as he said. She sought out Simon. "We didn't know, Simon. We thought it was real."

Simon laughed. "Then you're even more foolish than my father was." Another gasp.

The other officer reached Gerald and informed the couple they were being arrested for fraud.

"Not murder?" William asked. When the officer shook his head, William looked for Elsie. "Surely you can't still believe Cassidy killed him. It's obvious what happened."

"Is it? Please, do enlighten us," Gerald sneered. Even in handcuffs, the man was infuriatingly arrogant.

"You killed him, of course. Or your wife did. He found out about your little scam and threatened to expose you. This was his redemption, right Simon?"

"Sure. We'll go with that," Simon responded.

"But that's what you said. That's what you told Alex." William turned to her. "Right? This was Harold's redemption? That's what happened, isn't it?"

Alex nodded slowly, watching Simon, then turned towards the entrance. While the officers had made their way around the room, distracting nearly everyone, Elsie had sidled around her partner. Detective Monroe still couldn't get to Cassidy, though, because the older Devereaux was blocking her like a lineman.

"Stop right there, Elsie Monroe. You've had it out for my Cass for thirty-six years. I'm sorry you were hurt, and I'm sorry you didn't win that blasted talent show, but this has got to stop. You can't arrest someone simply because you don't like them. So what if she was prom queen and you were knocked up. That's not her fault. None of your life is her fault, so you better stop trying to punish her for it."

Alex's mouth dropped open. So did William's, and Cassidy's, and Reid's. Even Vanessa and Gerald stopped talking. Detective Washington hung back, arms crossed. He looked almost amused. Alex imagined his partner's single-mindedness had been frustrating.

Elsie stood stock still, dumbfounded. She looked shocked, but then she steeled herself with determination. She straightened her spine and looked down her nose at LuEllen, one of the only people she could do that to. LuEllen didn't buckle.

"Elsie." Cassidy spoke softly. "I'm sorry. I didn't know. If I had..."

"What? You'd have what? Decided not to read your stupid poem? Decided not to be so, so perfect?"

Cassidy didn't speak. Elsie contemplated the ceiling, then looked down at herself like she was taking inventory. She leveled her gaze at the woman she'd blamed for every bad thing in her life and held it. Then she seemed to come to a decision. She stepped back and looked at her partner. "You're right, Darrell. You've been right all along. I've allowed my personal experiences to get in the way of my job." Detective Washington visibly relaxed. Elsie switched back to Cassidy. "Don't leave town. And drive your own car. If I decide to arrest you, I will find you and trying to hide from me won't help."

Elsie stared at LuEllen until the older woman nodded, uncrossed her arms, and stepped aside. The detective motioned to the police officers who were still holding onto Vanessa and Gerald, then she pushed past Cassidy. Cassidy raised her arms and backed away from the door, which Elsie held open as the officers walked the doctors through the crowd.

Vanessa struggled the entire way. She craned her neck, seeking out Simon. "The medallion is real," she protested. "It's real, Simon, I swear."

"Shut. Up. Vanessa." Gerald said angrily. "Just shut up, for once in your life." The two continued arguing, Gerald accusing his wife of ruining it for them, and Vanessa telling her husband he was weak and a coward. Elsie stood with the door open, waiting for the uniformed officers to take the couple out of the building. She spoke to her partner. "You've got this?" When he nodded, she exited the museum. The door closed. Detective Washington stood next to it, his back against the wall, and scanned the room.

Slow clapping pulled everyone's attention towards the podium at the end of the hall. "Well done, Ms. Devereaux. Well done. You've managed to escape punishment, for now."

Cassidy refused to engage, but LuEllen puffed up. "Now you listen here–"

Simon laughed. "And well done to you as well, Miss LuEllen. Way to protect your baby sister. Too bad you couldn't have protected my father from her." He pointed the brass ball of his cane in Cassidy's direction. "Are you satisfied now? Is your vendetta complete? It wasn't enough for you to destroy his career. You had to destroy him."

Cassidy remained silent. She simply stared across the room. As people followed Simon's accusations, they moved back, unconsciously opening a swath between the two of them. She finally spoke. "I'm sorry about your father, Simon. And I'm sorry about the medallion."

He dismissed her apologies with a wave of his hand, the cane slicing through the air. "I couldn't care less about that blasted medallion. My father, however. But he's gone, and unlike some people, I trust the police will do their jobs." He leveled his gaze at Detective Washington. The man ignored him. "So, please, Ms. Devereaux. Enjoy the reception. I'm sure several of our guests will have questions about your discovery of the, quote unquote, *real* medallion. Take advantage of the limelight while you can, because I have no doubt this will be the last evening you may do so."

Simon cleared his throat, then addressed the room. "All of you, please enjoy as well. We have plenty of champagne and I believe I can hear our servers groaning with the weight of those appetizers. It's only kindness to relieve them of their burdens. And please, do not be concerned there's a murderer in your midst. Ms. Devereaux had a very specific vendetta against one man. The rest of you are safe." He laughed, then stepped away from the podium. The volume in the room gradually increased as the guests recovered from the shocking events and recounted them to each other.

Alex leaned against the wall next to the door to the courtyard. She and William hadn't moved since the police officers had handcuffed Gerald and Vanessa. They watched Cassidy, Reid, and LuEllen make their way towards them, the shorter woman leading the way. People stared and several tried to talk to them, but the trio continued until they reached their destination, which was the temporary bar. A line had formed as soon as Simon had stepped away from the podium, but they all cleared to make way for the determined woman. "You've got bourbon?" LuEllen demanded.

When the bartender nodded, she held up three fingers. "Neat," she said, then noticed Alex and William. "Make that five." She pulled out a twenty and put it in the tip jar, then handed out the whiskeys as he poured them. The five huddled together, silent until Cassidy cleared her throat.

"I propose a toast," she said. When they frowned, she smiled. "Here's to not getting arrested."

"I'll drink to that," William said.

Chapter 22

Alex pulled the valet ticket from her handbag and handed it to Reid. "I believe you'll be needing this." She accepted the ticket for her Outback from him and started to explain where he could find the truck.

"We saw it as we came in," he said. "How'd you manage that?"

"She has her ways," William said, eliciting laughter.

"I thought you might need a quick getaway," Alex explained. She searched Cassidy's face. "You OK?"

Cassidy shrugged. "I will be, as soon as they charge Vanessa with murder."

"You still think she did it?"

Reid nodded. "Who else? She had the biggest motive."

"What about Simon?" William asked. "I might not have thought so yesterday, but after tonight, I'm thinking that man's got some serious murdery vibes." He shivered, an exaggerated movement that sloshed the liquid in his glass.

"But why?" LuEllen asked. "He and Harold were patching things up. Harold even created that whole Garden of Death in there for him," she said, gesturing to the courtyard behind the door.

Alex turned to the door and sipped her bourbon. Through the walls, she pictured the lethal tree and its equally dangerous neighbors. William shielded his eyes. "Disco ball," he said. She turned back and gave him an indulgent smile.

"By the way, Ms. D, I want to compliment you on your magnificent choice of accessories. You sure know how to make an entrance."

Cassidy also smiled at William, but it was laced with sorrow. "I knew it was the only way to draw out Vanessa. I really do think she thought it was real, and that the story Talbot sold her was, too."

"Too bad she couldn't have stuck with that instead of trying to fool everyone into thinking they found it," Reid said.

"When we were at the dig site, I had the distinct impression that Vanessa wasn't a fan of actually digging," Alex said. "She kind of seemed like she loathed the job."

Reid nodded. "She does. Always did. That's why she tried to fake her research way back when." He nodded his head. "I knew it would catch up with her one day. But murder? I just don't know."

Cassidy sighed. "I know you don't want to think you were in love with someone capable of killing another human being, but I'm afraid that's what happened. You look for the good in people," she said, kissing him on the cheek.

"And so do you, Cass, no matter how many times you're proven wrong." LuEllen slammed the last of her bourbon and handed her empty glass to a passing server. "I don't know about you two, but I'm tired, and I'm tired of all these lookie-loos staring at us, wondering if you're going to suddenly go on a rampage."

Cassidy looked at Reid and he nodded. She bent down and hugged her sister tight. "Thank you," she said to Alex, looking over LuEllen's head.

"For what?" Alex replied. "Elsie's still coming after you."

"But not yet. And if we can prove Vanessa's guilty, not ever." Cassidy released her sister, then reached over to give Alex and William quick hugs.

Reid reached out to shake hands, but William pulled him in and gave him a kiss on the cheek. Reid kissed him back. William put his hand to the spot where Reid's lips had touched his skin. "I am never washing this cheek again—and if you knew my routine, you'd know how impressive that is."

"He's not lying," Alex smiled. "But I think I know who is," she said thoughtfully. She shook her head as if to bring herself back to the moment. She focused on Cassidy. "This isn't over, so keep in touch, please."

Cassidy nodded. LuEllen led the way towards the door and her sister and Reid followed, ignoring every attempt to talk to them on their way out. They left without a backwards glance.

William took a drink. "I knew tonight would be eventful, but I didn't realize it would be *that* eventful." Alex agreed. She stared at the crowd, not really seeing it. William waved his hand in front of her eyes. "Earth to Alex."

She shook her head, then focused as she saw Simon walking towards them, brushing off several guests who tried to speak to him. He reached Alex and William and pulled out his pocket watch. He spoke, but only to her. "I apologize, Ms. Paige. I seem to have missed our appointment. There was some important information you wanted to share with me?"

"It's already been shared," she said. "I was planning to let you know the medallion was a replica, and how I knew."

He began nodding in the middle of her sentence. "Thank you for your concern, but I knew it wasn't real. I've known since my father first told me about it."

"How?" William asked. Simon flicked his eyes towards him, but returned immediately to Alex.

"My poor father was rather naïve, and growing increasingly so. He was even considering starting a relationship with that 'Shrimp Shack' owner. She wasn't good enough for him. No one was, since mother... Anyway," he shook himself, "he'd worked with Dr. Sterling and Dr. Price for far too long. He was blinded by their credentials, her books, their somewhat celebrity status. He couldn't see what I could see."

"And that was?" William prompted again. Alex stayed silent, keeping her eyes on the botanist.

"That they were charlatans. Selling him a bill of goods and had been for years. That entire hall is filled with their supposed finds. He gave them legitimacy, and they took advantage of him."

"It seems they also gave him legitimacy."

Simon disagreed vehemently. "Absolutely not. He'd done that all on his own. After Ms. Devereaux," he sneered, "tried to destroy him with her little college thesis, he built himself back up. By the time those two frauds approached him, he'd had ten years of proving he was a scholar and a dedicated anthropologist. *They took advantage of him*," he repeated, raising his voice. He noticed heads had turned towards them, so he lowered it again. "I knew as soon as he told me about their latest find it was another fake with another fictional story."

"Why did you let him go through with this?" Alex finally spoke. She swept her arm to indicate she was talking about the opulent event.

Simon barked. "Let him? You think I could stop him? Oh no, Dr. Harold Baker may have been blind, but he was determined. When he wanted something, he got it."

"Including your return?"

He narrowed his eyes at her. "Yes. Including my return. You ask how I knew the doctors were conning my father. For the last twenty years, I've traveled the world. Outside the circle of sycophants they've built for themselves in the states, the doctors have quite a reputation. Father would send me email after email, begging me to come back, using those two as proof that he was back in the good graces of his peers. Damn fool.

"So, to answer your question," he continued, "I chose not to raise my suspicions. He wouldn't have entertained them anyway, and we'd been getting along so well. I really did appreciate what he created for me. It's enabling me to follow my vision."

Alex blinked, despite feeling nearly hypnotized by his intensity. William cleared his throat. "And what vision would that be?" he asked.

Simon flicked his eyes towards William again. This time he looked at him directly as he answered. "That is a long answer, and one that's longer than we have time for this evening, as I must be wrapping up this little shindig soon." He returned to Alex. "Earlier I mentioned I wanted to share my plans for this museum with you. Unfortunately, as I said, I missed our appointment," he chuckled. "Would tomorrow morning be acceptable? I realize it's a Sunday, but I believe it's worth violating a day of rest."

"Sure," she said. "We can be here by ten? Ten-thirty?" Alex glanced at William to confirm the time was acceptable.

"Ten-thirty would be preferable," he said, as she knew he would.

"No, that won't work. Ms. Paige, this is to be only you. I'm giving you an exclusive."

She inhaled so deeply it pinched her nostrils together. She did not like the idea of that one bit, but she needed to speak to him. "Fine. Let's make it eight then. I hope that won't be too early."

"Not at all, not at all. I will see you then." Simon reached for her hand and brought it to his lips. The kiss lingered longer than necessary. He ignored William completely, spinning on his heel and walking away.

Alex shuddered, then unconsciously wiped the back of her hand on her dress.

"I don't like this," William said.

"Nor do I, my friend. Nor do I."

It wasn't long before Simon announced the end of the event. He informed them since they'd already seen the medallion, or at least one of them, and heard the story, there was no need to continue the pretense that it was real. He asked them to consider the evening a memorial to his father, as Alex had earlier predicted he would.

"Thank you all for coming, and although it didn't turn out as planned, I hope you enjoyed yourselves. My father's final gift to you. Regarding plans, I'll take this opportunity to inform you the museum will be closed until further notice. I'll be making major changes, changes that have been a long time coming." With that, Simon walked to the corner and flipped the light switch, flooding the hall with bright light. Alex practically had to cover her eyes, the transition was so sudden.

"That was rude," William said. The bartender nodded agreement. Alex didn't respond, lost in her own thoughts. "Helloooo."

"Oh. Sorry. Yes, it was rude."

"I really don't like you meeting him tomorrow. He's half a bubble off plumb, if you ask me."

"I'll be fine. You know I can take care of myself."

"There's that feeling of invincibility again. I'll worry enough for the both of us. Tell you what. I'll text you at eight-fifteen–and yes, that means I will be getting up early, just for you. If you don't respond by eight-twenty, I'm sending in the cavalry."

"Cavalry?" Alex smiled.

"As in Cassidy, Reid, LuEllen, and myself. I figure the four of us can take him. Actually," he mused, "Reid could take him all by himself. The rest of us will just be there to enjoy the show."

The crowd thinned as people began filing out after Simon's abrupt announcement, enough so that Alex and William could also leave. They followed the slow-moving mass and lined up for the valet. "I'm serious," William said. "If I don't hear back from you post haste, we're coming to get you."

Alex agreed to William's plan, even if she thought he was being overprotective. "It'll be fine," she assured him. "He'll talk about his plans, I'll take notes and appear to be enthralled, and that'll be it. Really. The main reason I'm meeting him is to establish Vanessa's timeline yesterday morning and to find out if she entered the courtyard. If I can find that out, then Cassidy's off the hook."

Her statement was only partially true, but she knew if she told William what she'd really planned, he'd be on her doorstep waiting for her in the morning, no matter how early it was.

Chapter 23

Alex pulled into the parking lot, one of the few she'd entered in the last few days that was surfaced with asphalt. She sat for a moment. *Was this wise?* she questioned. *Was William right and she should have insisted he accompany her?* Too late now, she decided. She turned off the engine and checked her reflection in the mirror. She adjusted her baseball cap. It was going to be another cool, sunny day, so she'd repeated her outfit from the previous morning.

She wondered what Simon's plans could be, and figured it had to be something with his beloved plants. What a disturbing obsession, she thought, then tried to let it go. The reason people opened up to her was because of her empathy. If she allowed her disdain to be obvious, Simon would clam up like a, well, like a clam. She laughed softly to herself about her inability to think of a suitable simile. Even though her brain worked best in the mornings, she was a little loopy from all the drama since her arrival.

A sign on the door announced the museum's closing, "Until Further Notice." Alex knocked hesitantly, half-hoping the botanist wouldn't be there. Within moments, the heavy doors opened. Simon consulted his watch, an actual wristwatch this time. "You're punctual, Ms. Paige. So many people are not these days. My father always used to say, 'if you're on time, you're late.' Please, do come in." He opened the door wide and stepped back, inviting Alex to enter. He moved to close the door.

"Then I apologize for being late."

Simon turned as the door closed with a solid thud. All outside noise vanished and silence enveloped the hallway. "You're nothing of the sort. It was only a phrase he used to say. Frankly, I always thought it was quite pompous."

Alex gave him a small smile, then looked around the room. While last evening it had been transformed from the previous corridor into an elegant reception hall, this morning it was a veritable jungle. Plants crowded every space. Her jaw dropped, and she had to force herself to close her mouth. "This is marvelous," she exclaimed.

Simon beamed, the first genuine smile she'd seen on his face. "Isn't it? I knew you'd appreciate it."

"Did you sleep at all last night? You must have been working on this since everyone left."

He chuckled. "No no, I slept quite well, actually. I'd been collecting these since I returned. I've got a greenhouse out back where I can nurture them." He pointed to the ceiling. "I've installed grow lights so they can be displayed inside."

"I take it they're part of your plan."

"Beautiful and smart. Yes, they *are* my plan. This sad, tired homage to the dead will be transformed to a museum of the living." Simon strolled slowly down the hall, his hands clasped behind his back. He stopped in front of a plant that looked similar to Queen Anne's Lace. "Do you know what this one is?"

"Is that water hemlock?"

"Got it in one. Most impressive. Yes, this is water hemlock, not to be confused with poison hemlock, although they both are, of course, poisonous. And this one," he said, pointing to a plant with large black berries on the other side of the hallway, "is belladonna."

"A museum of the living, that causes death."

"Precisely. These are powerful organisms, capable of great beauty and of causing great pain. They sustain life, with their ability to convert carbon dioxide into oxygen, a necessary element to support humans. Yet some of them can kill in an instant."

"You're very passionate about this," Alex said. "Did your father know of your plans?"

He scowled. "He knew. Dismissed them out of hand. I could have my little courtyard, and grow my little plants in my little greenhouse, but *his* museum was for *serious* study, not for some childish hobby. He actually told me I would soon have to spend more of my time on the museum."

"Why was that?" Alex asked. She was suddenly quite glad William had arranged to check on her.

"Because he was dying," he said. "Oh, don't look so surprised. He'd been diagnosed with ALS. You saw how he'd rarely stay still? That's why. His effort to disguise his twitches."

"I'm so sorry."

Simon waved it off. "He could have lived for years. Yet he wanted me to train to take over his museum immediately." He opened the door to the courtyard and invited Alex in. They walked by a row of hazmat suits hanging above a line of folding metal chairs.

"Shouldn't we put one of those on?" she asked.

He looked her up and down. "Pants, long-sleeved shirt, hat. You're covered enough."

Alex doubted it. She followed him to a path that ran around the outside of the courtyard. Conflicting scents of apple, musk, and talcum assaulted her senses. She noticed many of the plants were shaped, trained by careful placements of stakes and zip ties. She had to get him talking about Vanessa. "Were you here when Dr. Sterling arrived yesterday morning?"

"I'm sure I was, but I didn't see her. I tended to avoid Vanessa and Gerald if at all possible."

"But with those windows into your father's office, you would have seen her, wouldn't you?"

Simon's eyes narrowed. "You're trying to get me to create a timeline for her, aren't you?" He put his index finger to his chin. "You really think she killed him."

"If she didn't, who did?"

"Why, Cassidy, of course. Isn't that what Detective Monroe believes?" He smiled slyly. "Someone might have pointed the detective in that direction."

Alex's eyes widened. *Oh, crap,* she thought. *I did it again.*

Simon nodded. "You see it now, don't you."

She gulped, nearly choking on her fear. She was isolated, in the middle of the Garden of Death, as LuEllen called it, with a man capable of murdering his own father. He walked by her towards the row of folding chairs. Alex stood, motionless, willing her phone to buzz. She wouldn't wait for William; she'd text him right away. "I see that your museum is going to be fabulous," she choked. "I'd love to hear more, but would it be possible to use the facilities first? I must have had too much coffee." She laughed nervously.

Simon swayed his head back and forth. "Nice try, but no, I don't think so. Turn around," he growled. She did as he ordered.

He yanked her arms behind her. She felt something hard and plastic cut into her wrists. *Zip ties*, she thought. He held her by the arm and pulled her backwards towards the wall, where he grabbed a chair. Simon marched her towards the manchineel tree. Alex resisted, pulling away from him. He dropped the chair and smacked her. She fell onto the stone walkway, her hat falling off and her face an inch from delicate pink flowers, which she knew to be oleander. She reared back and tried to scoot away from the deadly plant, but her bound hands made it impossible. Simon set the chair under the tree, then strode back to her, gripping her by the arms and viciously pulling her to her feet. He forced her to walk to the chair and sit down. He pulled more zip ties out of his back pocket and quickly secured her ankles to the legs of the chair. He noticed her hat on the ground. Walked over, picked it up, slapped it against his leg to shake any dirt off, then put it on her head.

He bent over and whispered in her ear. "I don't want you to die too quickly."

Alex began to panic. Her breathing increased until she knew she would hyperventilate if she didn't get it under control. She felt her pocket buzz. *William!* Why did they say he'd wait for five minutes? She could be dead by the time he got the other three together and drove to the museum. She moved her wrists to try to loosen her constraints, but her skin tore, still delicate from her radiation treatments, even though it had been months.

"Please, Simon. You don't have to do this. Isn't one death enough? Don't make it two."

He threw his head back and laughed. "You think my father was my first? It appears you're as naïve as he was. Now stop talking, or I will remove your hat and your shirt so you can feel the full power of la manzanilla de la muerte. That's what the museum will be called, by the way. *De la muerte.* Brilliant, isn't it?" He put his hands on his hips and surveyed the room.

"People know I'm here."

Simon mimicked holding a phone. "I'm sorry, Alex Paige? Yes, I invited her to join me for a private tour, but she never appeared. Of course, I'd love to let you into the museum, but I'm out of the country. Research, you see. Yes, of course, I'd love to hear where she took herself off to. Probably just went to the beach, hehe." He hung up the imaginary call and glared at her. "The museum is closed until further notice. There are no employees, no visitors, and," he looked at his watch, "in about five minutes, no Simon." He shook his head and gave her a pitying look while opening the door. "You should have let the police handle this."

The door burst open and slammed Simon against the wall. He fell into a pit of wolfsbane, their purple blooms swallowing him. His feet landed on the walkway. William jumped over them. Behind him, Detectives Monroe and Washington entered the courtyard, followed quickly by Cassidy and Reid. William raced to Alex. He pulled his pocketknife out of his cargo shorts, extracted the short blade, and cut her hands free. She leaned over and hugged him, sobbing. "Later," he said, then looked up at the deadly branches overhead. He cut the ties binding her ankles, then grabbed her hand and helped her walk away from the tree. When they were clear, he patted her shoulders and arms, like he'd done after her ride with LuEllen. He stopped when he got to her wrists, noting the torn skin where the ties had rubbed. He dropped her hand and walked to Simon, who now stood with his hands cuffed behind his back between the detectives. William punched him, knocking him back into the lethal flowers.

"Or, you could just leave him there," Reid suggested when Detective Washington bent down to help him up.

William walked back to Alex and took her hand, careful to avoid her raw skin, and pulled her out of the courtyard, out of the museum, and into the sun.

Epilogue

A gentle breeze caressed her cheeks. She held her sunglasses in one hand, letting the early evening sun warm her closed eyelids. Her chin tilted back. She inhaled the salty air. Sounds danced around her. A seagull. A child's squeal. The murmur of conversation. And laughter. So much laughter.

"Earth to Alex."

She opened her eyes and smiled at William, who was waving his hand in front of her. She put her sunglasses back on. Once her hand was free, William took it and examined the bandages that circled her wrists. Across from her, Cassidy spoke. "How are they?"

"A little tender, but they're not too bad. Anyone else's skin probably wouldn't have torn like that. I went kayaking about a month ago. Those paddles did a number on the web between my thumb and index finger before we even left the harbor." She spread the two digits to display them. "Already good as new."

"Did you hear?" LuEllen said as she lowered herself into a chair. They were on the beach at the first location of her eponymous restaurant, which was a little quieter than the new one. They sat around a large table covered in a red and white checkered plastic tablecloth. LuEllen poured herself a cup of her special sweet tea, then passed around the pitcher.

"Hear what?" Cassidy asked.

"Dr. Vanessa Sterling and Dr. Gerald Price have been officially removed from the Register of Professional Archaeologists for, and I quote, consistently betraying the ethics required of our profession. And, they were officially charged with fraud by the Gulf Shores police."

"Cheers to that," William said. They all raised their cups and tapped them to each other, each touch a dull click. "Not as satisfying as crystal, but it'll do."

"I heard Simon was officially charged with his father's murder, as well as a few other charges related to his attack on you," Reid said.

"Oh, he's getting charged with a lot more than that," LuEllen said. "After you told them he bragged about his father not being his first victim, Elsie and Darrell did a little investigating. That scoundrel left a string of bodies wherever he went. Turns out he was testing the poison of his beloved plants on real people."

They stared at her, shocked. William grabbed Alex's hand. "You're lucky to be alive. And oh yeah, about that—don't you dare ever do that to me again."

"I don't plan on it."

William eyed her. "Uh-huh."

"So tell me. How did you know to show up with these two instead of waiting for me to not reply, and how did you convince Detectives Monroe and Washington to join you?" Alex asked.

"Because you may have your spidey senses, but I've got a few antennae of my own. I didn't like Simon, and I certainly didn't trust him, especially after the way he slobbered all over your hand last night." William shivered. "I called Reid and told him you were too independent for your own good, and he said he knew a little something about that."

Cassidy grinned. "Who, me?"

"We all knew waiting was not an option, so they agreed to pick me up and we planted ourselves a block from the museum. At seven-thirty in the morning, I might add. *That* is how much I love you."

Alex leaned over and kissed him on the cheek. "And the detectives?"

"I might have told a wee little white lie." When she raised her eyebrows, William continued. "I told them I'd called over and over and you weren't picking up, but I knew you were at the museum with Simon—that part was true—and he seemed a little unhinged last night, which was also true. Basically, I begged and pleaded and finally said to them, fine, you don't go and she dies, it'll be all your fault and that's something you can't blame on Cassidy Devereaux."

Alex gasped. "You did *not* say that."

Cassidy nodded. "He absolutely did."

"So what's going to happen to the museum? Did Harold leave it to Simon?" William asked. They all turned towards LuEllen.

"Why are you looking at me?"

"Because if anybody knows, it's you, sis."

The older woman grinned. "Well... I did hear from a little bird that Harold put the museum in a trust for someone else, someone who is not Simon."

"And how would this little bird know this?" Cassidy asked.

"Because he might know someone who's a detective and who owes him a favor."

"Jacob?" Alex asked. "I had a feeling he was sweet on you."

LuEllen blushed. "Sweet on me? No, we're just friends who've known each other a long time. Oh, look, here's dinner." Two servers approached. One delivered plates and roll-ups containing flatware, and another put two large platters on the table. Skewers of chili and lime marinated grilled shrimp rested on a bed of couscous sprinkled with cilantro.

"Saved by crustacean," William winked, then grabbed a scoop of couscous, a kabob, and a lime wheel.

Cassidy also took a skewer, then bit into the shrimp. "This is delicious, Lu. New recipe?" Her sister, whose mouth was full, simply nodded. "So Harold didn't leave the museum to Simon. Who did he leave it to?"

LuEllen swallowed, took a big drink of her bourbon peach tea, and grinned. "You."

Cassidy choked. "What? Why would he do that? I'm the reason he lost his job."

Her sister wagged her finger. "None of that. *He* lost his job, remember? Jacob told me Harold, after being angry with you for years, decided he should thank you. He hated teaching. And he loved that museum, even as misguided as he was, he surely loved that museum. Thought you'd make a good steward." A wistful tone crept into her voice.

Cassidy drummed her fingers on the table. She looked at Reid. "We can get rid of any artifacts from Vanessa and Gerald."

"And display the ones we've discovered."

"And tell the true stories. We can tell what really happened." They grinned.

Alex looped her arm through William's as they walked along the beach in front of the condo building, carrying her shoes in her other hand. They walked on the hard packed sand where the water approached and retreated, over and over. They neared the alligator sculpture Zoe had been working on the day before. Wind and water had already smoothed it out, until all they could see was the vague outline. The sun was setting, glinting off the sparkling sand. "You know what's great about this place?"

"Besides that grilled shrimp?"

She shook her head. "As much as you love food, how you stay so thin is beyond me. Yes, besides that grilled shrimp. I love that you can see both the sunrise and the sunset from the same place."

William nodded. "That is pretty cool. So, you're seeing the village with Jacob tomorrow?"

"Yes. Cassidy and Reid are going to join me. Would you care to?"

"Nope. I'm cutting things short. Billy found the vandal, so I'm going to swing by to pick him up and we'll head to the Rockies for a few weeks."

Alex shook her head. "Only you would call a twenty-hour drive to Wisconsin 'swinging by' to pick someone up."

"What about you? After seeing the village, are you heading back? You had a pretty traumatic morning, so it'd be understandable if you wanted to get out of here."

Alex stopped and faced the Gulf. The water tickled her toes, and she wiggled them, burying them just a touch in the sand. "I can't believe that was only a few hours ago. It feels like a lifetime." A tear slid down her cheek. She let it fall. Should she go home? She buried her toes a little deeper. "Nope," she answered. "I'm staying right here. I've got a hot tub and drinks with umbrellas calling my name."

"No, really? Are you actually going to...?"

"Yes. I'm taking a vacation."

I hope you enjoyed spending time with Alex, William, and the entire cast. Follow their next adventures in *Ruin on the River*, where Alex exposes dark ambitions and bitter rivalries in this thrilling cozy mystery set in the mountains of Western North Carolina. thelocaltourist.com/ruin

BONUS: save 20% on Alex Paige's adventures at theresas books.com! Use code BETRAYED20.

For even more Alex, find out how her travel writing career began—with a crime, of course! She's barely off the plane for her first research trip when she encounters the police. Will the Sonoran Desert, and her new career, prove too hot for her to handle? Visit thelocaltourist.com/go/stolen/ to get your free short story, *Stolen on the Salt River*.

Recipe
Grilled Shrimp with Citrus-Chili Marinade

If you thought their celebratory shrimp dish at LuEllen's Shrimp Shack sounded delicious, here's the recipe so you can try it out for yourself.

Serves 4

Ingredients:

- 1 pound large shrimp, peeled and deveined

- 3 tablespoons olive oil

- Zest and juice of 1 medium orange

- Zest and juice of 1 lime

- 1 clove garlic, diced

- 2 teaspoons chili powder

- Chipotle powder to taste

- 1/2 teaspoon cumin

- Salt and black pepper to taste

- Fresh cilantro leaves for garnish

Instructions:

1. In a bowl, whisk together the olive oil, orange zest and juice, lime zest and juice, chili powder, cumin, garlic, salt, and black pepper.

2. Coat the shrimp with the citrus-chili marinade and let them marinate in the refrigerator for about 20-30 minutes (save some in reserve for suggested serving below)

3. Thread the shrimp onto skewers. Soak wooden skewers in water for about 30 minutes before using to prevent burning.

4. Preheat the grill to medium-high heat.

5. Grill the shrimp skewers for 2-3 minutes per side, or until they are opaque and cooked through.

6. Remove the shrimp from the grill and serve immediately, garnished with fresh cilantro leaves.

Serving Suggestion

Save approx. 1/2 cup of marinade. While the shrimp is marinading, thinly slice red onions and dice cucumbers. Mix into marinade with about a tablespoon of cilantro leaves. To serve, mix shredded lettuce or cabbage into your doctored marinade. Distribute in plates or bowls and place shrimp kabobs on top, then sprinkle with cilantro and crumbled queso fresco. Light, delicious, and healthy!

You could also serve your Grilled Shrimp with couscous, rice, or grilled vegetables, or a lovely salad.

Also By Theresa L. Carter

As Theresa L. Carter

Alex Paige Books 1-5
Get the first five Alex Paige adventures!
Peril on the Peninsula
Revenge in the Rockies
Betrayed at the Beach
Ruin on the River
Chaos in the Canyon
Menace at the Marina

As Theresa L. Goodrich

Two Lane Gems, Vol. 1
Turkeys are Jerks and Other Observations from an American
Road Trip
Two Lane Gems, Vol. 2
Bison are Giant and Other Observations from an American Road
Trip
Living Landmarks of Chicago
Planning Your Perfect Road Trip

Show Me Shipshewana
A Guide to Indiana Amish Country
Discover Geary County, Kansas
Nature, History, and Hometown Hospitality in the Sunflower
State

Publisher / Contributor

Midwest Road Trip Adventures, 2nd Edition
Midwest State Park Adventures

Author Note

Alex Paige visits a lot of real destinations. She also visits a lot of places that are entirely made up. Dr. Baker's Gulf Coast History and Archaeology does not exist, nor does LuEllen's Shrimp Shack (either location). However, if you've got a hankering for smoked tuna dip, I suggest heading to LuLu's. The condo Alex stayed in? Also real. It's modeled after Turquoise Place, and yes, their balconies are big enough for pacing *and* a hot tub.

One of my favorite real places is the ancient canal, although I haven't seen it (yet). An amateur archaeologist by the name of Harry King has been instrumental in preserving this piece of history. Another wonderful spot is Bon Secour National Wildlife Refuge, although I have no idea if teenagers in Gulf Shores used it as a sort of Lover's Lane.

Zoe Monroe is modeled after a young woman who really does build sand castles for a living. Speaking of sand, you may be wondering: does it really sparkle?

Yes, yes it does.

Acknowledgments

The first thing I want to acknowledge is that writing acknowledgments is hard. You don't want to forget anybody, and no matter how many people you thank, you know you've left someone out.

Part of the reason writing acknowledgments is hard is because writing a book is a long process, even when you write fast. I began writing Betrayed at the Beach in April. Three months later, I wrote "The End," and that was with a two month break in between for work and moving. Yet, it's still a long process. How many projects do you tackle that take thirty days, sixty days, or even years? A lot happens between start and finish, including Life, and it's easy to forget a few things along the way.

The publication date of my first novel, Peril on the Peninsula, was August 13, 2022. The publication date of my third? August 14, 2023. I didn't plan this. Alex and William did, and I just write what they tell me.

Alex Paige appeared nearly fully formed on October 28, 2021. I had committed to participating in my first NaNoWriMo (National Novel Writing Month). I'd planned to write a novel about Chicago, but then I realized I'd be so focused on research I'd never get it written. Then, one morning, an Aha! moment. And there she was.

So I guess my first acknowledgment goes to NaNoWriMo, because without that commitment, I don't know how long it would have taken me to finally sit down and write a novel. I knew I was going to, but that gave me a date.

My second is to Gulf Shores and Orange Beach Tourism. I visited in late February/early March of 2021. This was not a vacation. It was work. I was teaching a writing workshop for the Midwest Travel Network. The workshop was originally scheduled for October of 2020, but both COVID and a hurricane caused a delay.

I also had a personal wrinkle. Cancer. By the time the dates for the rescheduled workshop rolled around, I was in the middle of my second round of chemotherapy. We were still in the middle of a pandemic. I had no immune system to speak of. Oh, and the week before we were set to leave? I found out what I thought was a spray of whiteheads on my face was actually shingles. I was hesitant to go, but my oncologist told me, repeatedly, that my mental health was important, too.

We did it. Ford loaned me an Expedition Platinum Max. We named her Penny, after my grandmother. "Max" is an apt descriptor. We fit a full-sized futon in the back. Because we couldn't stay in hotels or eat at restaurants or be around people, period (no immune system, and no vaccines yet), we took our time driving down, sleeping at campgrounds in the back of this luxury SUV.

Then the conference. Students traveled from all over. We wore masks. We kept our distance. I taught by open doors; fresh air from the Gulf circulated through the large room. With those precautions, despite four days and three nights of relative togetherness, not a single person got sick, including me.

This is a long way of saying thank you, to Gulf Shores, to Midwest Travel Network, to Ford, and to Dr. Singh, who made an adventure possible and unexpectedly inspired the setting for this book.

I also want to acknowledge so many friends and readers who told me how excited they were to read Alex's next shenanigans, and were gracious when I had to push the publication date back due to our move. This is where I know I'll miss names, and I know I can't include everyone: Karen Gill, Shelly Harms, Lori Helke, Veronica Bareman, Bek Rebich, Sean Berry, Larry and Carol Pratt, Amy Zagroba, Henry Brandt, Nancy Lange, Susan Tyson, Debbie Huber, Sarah Grimm (who signed up to be on my ARC team while on vacation in Italy!), Julie Diebolt Price, Heidi Kohz, Cindy Ladage, Mary Petri, and so many more. THANK YOU!!!

And to my parents. My tight deadline meant Dad couldn't dive in with his usual detail, but he helped shape the beginning. Mom read, edited, re-read when I made changes, including adding whole chapters, edited, pointed out errors and inconsistencies, and generally made this book better, as she always does. She put other things aside to help make this book the best it can be. Thank you.

Tatiana—my insane timeline prevented you from editing this book, but I heard your voice in my head with every line (paying special attention to pronouns, commas, and one-sentence paragraphs). I hope I made you proud.

And, to Jim. It's my tenth book and you've been here for every one, cheering me, feeding me, and being supremely patient with me, especially since I've started writing mysteries and now frequently talk about the finer points of how to murder someone. I love you.

Thank you to everyone who's given their valuable time to these books. I hope they gave you a fun escape, and maybe even inspired a new destination.

Theresa L. Carter

About Theresa L. Carter

Theresa's one of those voracious readers who grew up with her nose in a book and the desire to write her own. That took some time, as she spent years telling people where to go as a full-time travel writer before making it happen when she was 47 (because you're never too old to start). That book, *Turkeys are Jerks and Other Observations from an American Road Trip*, lit a long-dormant fire, and she's continued to write and publish travel books at a rapid pace ever since. She still wanted to write novels, though, and after a breast cancer gut punch, decided at age 51 not to wait any more. Alex Paige sprung out of her head, Athena-like, and hasn't left her alone since.

When Theresa's not telling people where to go or being told by Alex and friends what to write, she's reading (of course), learning, cooking, figuring out how to spend as much time outside as possible, or annoying her husband.

And sometimes, all of the above.

You can find Theresa on social media @theresastoryteller and at theresasbooks.com

www.ingramcontent.com/pod-product-compliance
Lightning Source LLC
Chambersburg PA
CBHW021708190726
48289CB00008B/2425